HER BODY SEEMED TO FLOAT . . .

The penetrating warmth of his hands moved lightly and swiftly over her shoulders and up her neck. Her body swayed with them, yearning for more.

"Oh, baby, baby," he sighed.

Her fingers reached up to ruffle his hair. She was in ecstasy . . . until a yelp from Rocky, who had settled at their feet, brought her suddenly to her senses. Hastily pulling her robe back around her, she zipped it in a defiant motion and looked away from Matt's startled eyes.

"I'm sorry . . ." she gasped. "Please go . . . ! This is a terrible mistake!"

A QUESTION OF TRUST

Dorothy Ann Bernard

A CANDLELIGHT ECSTASY ROMANCE™

Published by
Dell Publishing Co., Inc.
1 Dag Hammarskjold Plaza
New York, New York 10017

ISBN: 0–440–17315–9

Printed in the United States of America
First printing—April 1982

Dear Reader:

In response to your continued enthusiasm for Candlelight Ecstasy Romances™, we are increasing the number of new titles from four to six per month.

We are delighted to present sensuous novels set in America, depicting modern American men and women as they confront the provocative problems of modern relationships.

Throughout the history of the Candlelight line, Dell has tried to maintain a high standard of excellence to give you the finest in reading enjoyment. That is and will remain our most ardent ambition.

Anne Gisonny
Editor
Candlelight Romances

To my husband Bernie

A QUESTION
OF TRUST

CHAPTER ONE

The aroma of the pine forest wafted in through the high screened windows of the A-line chalet and created a sense of luxurious, pleasant cacophony as the birds and creatures of the woods greeted each other in the early morning. Irene Malone moaned in her sleep and rolled her lean, graceful body from a relaxed fetal tuck into a swirling sprawl across her wide bed. The silk and lace of her nightgown found new places to accentuate as her arms went up to frame the tumble of wild red hair falling about her head and shoulders. Unconsciously she reached out her hand, searching the empty space next to her. Slowly gaining momentum, her movements grew more frantic until suddenly she sat up, wide awake yet dazed, not sure of her surroundings.

"Oh my God," she sighed, her head dropping forward into her hands. When would she ever get used to it? When would she wake up, not reaching for him?

Wrapping her arms around herself in a protective gesture, she slowly began to get up. Tossing her red hair back, she slid into a silky robe matching her gown and pushed

11

her feet into satin mules. Tying the belt snugly around her slim, firm waist she wandered toward the window and breathed in her surroundings, seeking the therapy that they always provided. She took several deep breaths and immediately felt better. Slowly and languidly she stretched her body with a sinewy feline grace before allowing herself to glance back toward the wide, disheveled bed, but it was no use. The memories still came. She couldn't avoid or control them as they swept over her, exposing her to the secreted pockets of anguish she had worked so hard to conceal and forget. First, from nowhere, she remembered his dark tousled head and smiling eyes and the hours and hours of lovemaking when time had been nonexistent; his touch, the trailing fingers whispering over her body; the murmurs and secrets that belonged only to them; and then, the horror and heartsick disgust when she learned she had been betrayed. Over and over again she saw him, in her mind, with another woman, sharing their secrets in an anguished and emotional conflagration. She couldn't bear it. She just couldn't handle it, yet, God, how she ached for him. She clutched herself and felt the tears coming to temper her pain.

"Stop it! Stop it!" she said to herself as she pulled herself angrily toward the kitchen. "You've got to stop this! Just once, you have to get up without this. You can do it," she continued sternly, "you are strong enough to put this behind you. . . ."

Suddenly, in the midst of her self-admonition and pep talk, she heard a terrible racket. Something on her porch was literally ripping the wood on her screen door apart. All of her senses were immediately alert as she ran toward the noise.

Hurrying through the chalet, clutching her flimsy nightclothes about her, she was alerted to yet another noise. Gravel was crunching and popping, accompanied by the sounds of a big engine gunning its way up her drive. At the same time something heavy scrambled away from her door. She heard the scrabble of claws on wood, but by the time she got the door open and ran through it, whatever was there was gone. She was used to visits from the creatures in the forest, especially raccoons, but as she surveyed the scratched and shredded lower panel of her screen door it was obvious something much larger had done this. She shivered. The thought of a bear cub with its mama not far behind quickly crossed her mind.

"Morning, miss."

Whirling around, Irene saw that a big oversized pickup truck with bulging trail tires had appeared. Its powerful motor was idling impatiently. The big, dark-haired man driving it leaned forward.

"Sorry to bother you so early in the morning." He paused momentarily as his dark eyes crinkled and appraised her in a practiced, macho way.

Self-consciously, Irene wrapped her robe a little tighter, which, contrary to her modest motivations, simply enhanced her trim figure in a voluptuous, almost risqué way. She was caught completely off guard.

The man's eyes continued to dance over her appreciatively as his deep voice went on with his interrogation. "I was just wondering if by any chance you might have seen my dog?" His voice was warm and friendly with a hint of laughter in it as he swung his big frame from the truck and began to amble toward her, obviously amused by her discomfiture.

Instinctively Irene's hand went protectively to her breasts. Then, thoroughly embarrassed, she came to her senses and quickly pulled the door open so she could scamper inside. Her momentary disorientation was now replaced by indignation. Already out of sorts thanks to that aggravating dream and the shock of hearing her door being ripped apart, she was in no mood to deal with some ogling stranger who happened to catch her in her nightgown on her own front porch.

"I'm sorry," she said crossly, "the kennel is not open until ten A.M. You'll have to come back then."

"I don't need anything from your kennel," he said in mock exasperation as he continued to look her over.

Irene could feel herself beginning to blush. Angrily, she slammed the door in his face and quickly turned the dead bolt. Going over to the screened window next to it, she repeated in a now thoroughly irritated, but calculatingly calm voice, "The kennel is *not* open until ten A.M., and I'd appreciate it if you would just leave. I'm not dressed."

As she leaned over to talk through the window the low neckline of her filmy gown hinted at a tantalizing cleavage, all of which was quite visible to the stranger as he glanced at her through the screen.

"That," he said sarcastically, as he turned to leave, "is quite obvious." He angrily leaped the rail with athletic grace, jumped into the truck, and gunned the motor all in one seemingly simultaneous motion. Irene stood motionless, silently seething as the big truck disappeared down the lane.

The events of the past few moments had left sections of her brain in various states of detached limbo—as though some had been left behind and needed to catch up. For a few stunned seconds she searched, seeking some cohesive factor that would bring them all together again and restore her to normalcy. Remembering why she had come into the room in the first place, her glance traveled to the door and she began to move toward it to take another look at the damage. As her hand reached to turn the dead bolt she heard a crash. Something was on the back porch. She ran back and then came to a stunned halt.

"What in the . . ." she gasped as she looked out the back

door in shock. One of the macrame plant hangers she had spent hours making was demolished, its contents strewn all over the porch. A gaping hole was being made in the screen as the white snout of a medium-sized, muscular dog, from a breed she didn't readily recognize, continued its demolition with the obvious intention of coming in. She gasped again as she heard the wood literally crunch and crumble in his huge, powerful jaws.

"You stop that!" she shouted in a staccato voice as she clapped her hands and stomped her feet to shoo him away.

Hearing her, the animal stopped and whined before stepping back and sitting lopsided with one hind leg under him. He raised his great brute head and tilted it at a quizzical angle toward her. His eyes were gentle, but mischievous and imploring. He was obviously still a puppy. As his great mouth split into a panting grin, Irene stepped closer and saw that his ears had been cropped and they still had stitches in them. The stitches were overdue for removal, which was why his head looked so big and unnatural. He also had what looked like a scrape on the side of his snout and rear hip, several days old. His short white coat was dulled with street grime and mud.

Seeing him in this "sad sack" comedic pose, she was suddenly relieved and all of the tensions of the morning dissipated with her laughter.

"Where in the world have you come from?" she jested, her hands on her hips. "You've sure made a mess for me!"

The dog whined and wriggled in response, thumping a little short stub tail, anxious for affection, but hesitant to leave his sitting stance. About that time, Buffy, Irene's ten-month-old golden cocker spaniel, came tearing in from the back where he had been occupied around her boarding kennel. She could hear her tenants now, and from the sound of their barks and howls all of them were hungry.

"Well, come on," she said to the big oaf of a dog as she reached for the door. "I guess one more won't make that much difference. Someone must have lost . . . oh, no!" she groaned as she remembered the arrogant dark stranger she had just chased away. She hadn't allowed him to leave a description, but the two incidents were a little too coincidental not to be related. "Well," she said resignedly, as she brushed her hair back, "he'll probably be back. Cute," she said curtly, "very cute! I can hardly wait."

She reached out to pet the dog. "I'd better get you something to eat before you destroy my whole house." Pausing again, while once more appraising the sturdy, unusual conformation and structure of the dog, she mused, "Looks like you might have gotten clipped by a car, too. Some owner you've got—you probably fell out of that big truck!"

She named him Rocky almost unconsciously. Then she stopped and stooped down to take another, more careful look at the dog as slowly the truth dawned on her. She looked at the ears and the scratches on the snout again as a curse of disgust escaped. "My God, you're a pit bull! An American pit bull terrier," she exclaimed, "and that sorry son of a so-and-so who is looking for you is training you to fight!"

Pit dogfighting was one of the most covert, heinous activities of the area, patronized by many locals who felt it was a much maligned sport as equally noble as bullfighting was to the Spanish, certainly no worse than boxing.

Buffy had continued his racket and in a flash, before Irene could stop him, he was out the door lunging toward the much larger dog.

"Buffy," she screamed, but he paid her little mind. Seeing the contrast in their sizes made Irene afraid. If the pit bull had had any serious conditioning at all he would instinctively tear the little dog to bits. She held her breath

16

as Rocky slowly stood up and they both went into the stiff, anxious nose-to-nose appraisal, normal for all dogs meeting for the first time. To her relief they broke their stance, gave a playful growl, and tumbled toward each other, quick and fast friends.

"You are a weirdo," she said as she patted Rocky. "You don't act like any dog I've ever seen and I thought I'd seen them all."

Continuing to pat the dog, Irene walked toward the kitchen while trying at the same time to avoid stumbling over Buffy, who was darting in and out and around them, grabbing and tugging at Rocky playfully. She went to the sink to fill the tea kettle with water for her morning coffee and looked out toward her pride and joy, the boarding kennel she had built along with this house after the divorce.

She had left Miami deliberately looking for a change of scene and found this wonderful contrasting paradise with a little of everything in the Florida panhandle. She was located just on the outskirts of the small, picturesque tourist town of Cramdon, which boasted beautiful white sand beaches still largely uncontaminated by commercialization. Heading due north out of the town you were soon in deep south backwoods, embroidered with wild flowers and pine trees. Summers were hot and humid but tempered by the beach. Winters were just nippy enough for a fireplace, interspersed with glorious sunny days when only a sweater was needed and sometimes not even that. She loved the forest and beach equally during that time of the year, when all was usually quiet and few people were around to intrude on her reveries as she walked deep in thought and wonder.

As she opened cans of food and dished it into large dog dishes, Irene took another look at Rocky's ears. Her face hardened and her stomach began to churn. They were

17

cropped extremely short and close, a practice that she had heard was often utilized by the dogfighters when the dog was slated for the pit. She was almost sick with disgust as she took another look at the scratches on the dog's snout and remembered hearing locals discuss how they often used live kittens and other small creatures for bait to develop the dog's inbred latent aggressive tendencies.

Then she remembered the snide, arrogant stranger and the gun rack in his truck. It fit. He was the stereotype of the kind of man out to make a buck at the expense of an animal's life and pain. She noted that Rocky was without collar or tags and in an instant made a decision that was bound to immerse her in a raging conflict. She was not about to let that man have this dog, whether he was the owner or not. This was one dog that was not going to kill or be killed in a secret dogfighting pit.

She conveniently allowed herself only a surface comprehension of what she had just decided, refusing to appreciate fully the consequences of such an action. It was a determination that seemed to mesh with the general aggravation of the morning thus far. As she continued to move about the kitchen she was irritated with herself as she thought about her morning experiences before she discovered Rocky.

It had been more than a year now since she had struck out on her own and she had proven herself to be a very shrewd businesswoman—more than capable of taking care of herself. At twenty-six, she had taken a hobby and interest in animals and turned it into a rewarding and profitable career. Beginning with two dogs and a little bit of seed money borrowed from her mother, she had soon acquired this land and built the small chalet and kennel, something she had always wanted to do.

The chalet was furnished in her own cozy but elegant style, accented with articles from her pastimes, hooked

18

rugs, afghans, and woven seat covers on rockers found indoors and out. She felt safe and secure in it, and especially enjoyed it when the mood struck her to make bread or soup. Her kennel's reputation was well-established, and she often had a waiting list for weekends and holidays because her facility was clean and well-managed, which mirrored her care and compassion not only for animals but people as well.

Walking to the phone, she was about to call the local humane society but quickly realized that would be counterproductive if she were to make a legitimate claim on the dog. She wondered if she had space in the kennel and then realized that was no good either. She couldn't take the risk of the dog's not having shots, which could endanger all of her boarders, and even though he was friendly with Buffy she still didn't know how he would react with the other dogs. No, Rocky would have to stay here with Buffy, as another personal pet.

"Oh, brother," she said out loud, "I don't know how I'm ever going to pull this off." The straight and narrow in her bridled at this deception, but her heart told her she was doing the right thing. With each passing minute she was becoming more attached to Rocky and more committed to protecting him in any way she could.

It's too bad, she thought, that the only chancre in this area is the love of this illegal, covert activity. It wasn't loved by everyone, to be sure, but there seemed to be a fierce pride even among those who decried it to protect those who indulged in it.

Actually, though, in spite of this one dark spot, Irene was very happy with her choice of home. She had at heart always been an old-fashioned girl, drawn to things of the past, enchanted by the romance of earlier times. She didn't fully realize, however, the extent of her morality until after the divorce, which had been a painful and degrading experience. Stung by accusations that she was cold and old, no longer fun, from someone to whom she had yielded the nectar of her soul, and then admonished because of her inability to forgive and forget, it had ultimately become an act of self-respect that she had to endure.

Hurt and wounded, she had made up her mind to throw out all of her romantic notions and embrace the new morality with enthusiasism, only to find that she simply could not function outside the secure confines of a loving commitment. And yet, she was a deeply passionate, fiery person, and while she couldn't forgive her former husband she would always miss him, and mornings such as this morning would probably never go away. In reality it had been a relief to leave the fast pace of the big city with its demands of one-night stands, sans involvement, for the peace and tranquillity that she usually found here.

General chaos greeted Irene as she stepped into the kennel. All of her canine charges competed to be the first to attract her attention. Their barks echoed over the clean smooth walls and floors accented by stainless steel and fiberglass fixtures. Each of the animals had its own indoor-outdoor run or secluded accommodations according to their needs. She had a full house today. Her helper had already arrived and was well into the morning scrub down. Several pick-ups were scheduled, so she began preparations for their baths, something she always included with her service.

As she finished up Irene noted that 10:00 A.M. had come and gone with no sign of the stranger. The work in the kennel had momentarily relieved her of her troubled thoughts. Now that she had calmed down she realized that she really didn't know if Rocky belonged to him or not. In her angry impatience Irene knew she had been rude, but the memory of his arrogant insolence following so soon after that irritating dream quickly sparked her indignation all over again.

"But then, it really doesn't matter," she said to herself haughtily. She was determined, more so than ever, not to give the dog up. There was no doubt in her mind that somebody had slated him for the dogfight pit and she just couldn't allow that to happen. Secretly, though, she rather hoped the owner was not that arrogant redneck. Somehow the thought of tangling with him left her decidedly uncomfortable.

Later in the afternoon, Irene realized that she had to get Rocky his shots and have him checked over not only because she had strict rules about that at the kennel, but more importantly the tags and city license would give her a legitimate claim to the animal. She gathered up Rocky and took him to Dr. Quigley, the local veterinarian.

The doctor looked at her quizzically when he saw the dog. "Expanding your interests?" he queried. "This fella is quite a change of pace for you, isn't he?"

Irene, usually bubbly and friendly with this man, found his questions, combined with her concern, confusion, and an unmistakable sense of guilt, almost impertinent. "No, not really," she said tightly. She was nervous and anxious to return home.

With each succeeding minute the implications of her situation became more apparent, and Irene found herself growing deeply concerned for the safety of Rocky and her ability to protect him. She must get him home, into a safe place where no one would notice him. She didn't know how she was going to accomplish that. One thing you could not do with Rocky was ignore him.

The doctor continued the examination in silence, glancing at Irene periodically with a puzzled and concerned expression on his face. With a sigh he administered the protective shots against rabies, distemper, and parvo to the dog and removed the stitches. Rocky barely noticed as he panted away good-naturedly, impervious to the tension in the room. He looked about mischievously and tried to swipe their faces with his big pink tongue. The doctor filled in the vaccination certificates and Irene grabbed them. Tossing only a perfunctory "So long, I'll see you later" behind her, she hurried out the door.

A few moments later they were safely home, and Irene went about her usual chores after leaving Rocky in the house. She was in the kennel only a few moments when she heard another crash just like the one she had heard that morning. Running, she burst through the door just in time to see Rocky and Buffy dragging one of her favorite plants around the room, strewing potting soil all over the place.

"Oh, no!" she cried. "What is it with you? Have you got a thing about wood and macrame or something?" She was standing in spread-eagled exasperation, her hand to her head.

"Have you got problems of some kind, ma'am?"

Irene whirled around. The dark stranger from the morning stood in the doorway. He was a tall, dark-haired man, probably in his early thirties. She hadn't taken time to calculate his age earlier. His hair flowed back in raven waves from a widow's peak and framed an intense, handsome masculine face with dark, brooding eyes. Right now they were pretending to be friendly. He was big, seeming all the more so because he was attired in rugged woodsman's clothes—red and black plaid shirt with rugged jeans and boots. He had a hat in his hand as he looked down at her.

Still affected by her morning encounters and her covert activities, Irene was completely unnerved by his unexpected appearance. She looked up at him in total confusion as she stopped in midmotion. Her hand was just beginning to move her tumbled hair back from her face.

"Problems? No . . . no, I don't have any problems," she stammered. "I'm just getting after my dogs here—they've been a little rambunctious."

His eyes were electric and seemed to pierce through her. "Your dogs? Is that big white one your dog?" he questioned with authority.

She answered him much too fast. She was not very practiced at deceit. "Yes, he's my dog," she said nervously. She moved protectively toward Rocky and pulled him to her as she sank into a chair.

"Well, ma'am," he said in a puzzled tone, "I don't mean to differ with you, but you see, you know that I was looking for my dog this morning, and I have proof that that's *my* dog."

"No," Irene raised her chin and said firmly, "no, that's not possible. He is *my* dog." Seeking to dismiss him, she looked around. "Whatever would make you think such a thing?"

His jaw clenched as he drew a quick breath and attempted to answer her, but she interrupted him. In spite of her resolve Irene was finding it difficult to meet his challenge. "What are you doing in my house?" she demanded, losing patience. "I didn't ask you in."

"Now just a minute," he said, somewhat exasperated by her behavior. "I'm sorry, I didn't mean to just barge in, but it sounded like you were having some trouble. Now can we just settle down and start all over again?"

There was a little lopsided grin playing on his lips, but his eyes were serious and somehow commanded her to calm down, which was in itself somewhat infuriating.

"My name is Matt Davis," he said, "and I've lost a dog just like that one a couple of days ago. He was due to have the stitches in his ears out about a week ago and I just

23

didn't get around to it. I was taking him to get it done when he disappeared from my truck. He's a good dog, a registered American pit bull terrier, and I paid a lot of money for him."

Irene looked out and saw again the big, powerful oversized truck, the kind the local macho types gloried in riding around in. She looked at him with an expression of obvious distaste. In the meantime, Rocky had become aware of the man's presence and to Irene's horror began to whine and whimper trying to reach him.

"You see," he said, "that's my dog. Doc Quigley told me he thought you had one just like him."

"Well, he is *not* your dog," she said with emphasis, "and you cannot have him!"

"Now, just a minute," he countered in kind, his cool beginning to slip a bit, "I have proof, registration papers— you know I was looking for him . . ."

She flew back at him, a picture of controlled, fiery consternation. "I know what you want to do with him," she said in contempt, "and I refuse to let that happen!"

He looked at her, shocked for just a second, and then he purposely willed himself to relax, almost matching her contempt as his eyes traveled over her poised and arrogant body, clad in tailored jeans and fashionable shirt, punctuated by her wild mane of red hair.

"Oh, you do, do you?" he said softly in mock serenity. "And just what might that be?"

"You know exactly what I'm talking about," Irene said in low, deadly tones, "and as far as I'm concerned you'd just better get out of my house before I call the sheriff and have you thrown out!"

"Okay, okay," he said, still speaking softly, "we'll take care of this legally."

His eyes locked with hers as if they were in mortal deadly combat. She glued hers to his and refused to flinch as she pointed to the door. As the seconds ticked by she felt herself slowly growing warmer as an insidious blush began to creep over her.

"Out!" she shouted. Suddenly Irene was so angry she found herself rushing toward him. With both arms she made an effort to push his bulk through the door. "Just get out!" she cried.

She was no match for him and she could feel herself losing control. What had gotten into her? She was almost provoked to physical violence. Had her fear for the animal along with her guilt over the day's activities stripped her of her usual ability to handle any situation competently with tact and diplomacy? To further complicate things her body was suddenly betraying her. When her fingers touched his chest and felt the wild strength there she had an exciting, trembling reaction to this terrible man; a man who, if she were not careful, would most surely take Rocky away to use him in some terrible and heinous way.

Slowly he stilled her hands and stepped away, his eyes never leaving her face although his tanned face had whitened just a bit. Without another word he turned and left, slamming the door after him.

Irene was repulsed over her response to him, but as a dark knot began to form in the pit of her stomach she also, for some ridiculous reason, felt a sense of regret over the way he had left.

Rocky whined at her feet and she sighed. For some strange reason the dog had grown exceedingly quiet during their loud altercation and now he looked up at her quizzically. Patting him, she pulled herself up and began to clean up the mess, wondering what she was going to do next.

CHAPTER TWO

The squeal of tires and gravel flying announced the arrival of Matt Davis's powerful pickup truck the next morning. Following close behind was the car of the local sheriff.

Buffy and Rocky set off an immediate commotion, which was soon echoed by all of her kennel residents as Irene rushed to the window to see what was going on. The hard slam of the truck door followed by Matt's quick, determined steps indicated that his mood was less than congenial, as he landed heavily on her deck and began pounding impatiently on the front door of the chalet.

"Hold your horses there, fella," said the sheriff, who was having a hard time keeping up. "We aren't going to a fire. Now you just settle down," he admonished sternly. "This matter will be taken care of, but it's going to be taken care of right."

Matt was paying him little heed as Irene went to open the door. She was clad in trim jeans and a fitted Western-style plaid shirt. She had just finished brushing her long hair and was in the process of tying the ribbon she used to sweep it back from her face while she went about her morning kennel chores when she heard the noise outside. Thanks to the exhausting events of the day before she had, almost unbelievably, slept well. She looked and felt fresh, her normal composure having once again returned in contrast to her emotional outburst and nervousness of the day before.

"Good morning, Sheriff." Irene spoke directly to him in her brightest voice, giving Matt only a cursory nod.

She was a picture of morning sunshine, and the sheriff quickly noted the coziness and attractivness of her home and the way she fit into it so naturally. Buffy and Rocky fell over themselves trying to greet the visitors. In the midst of all this confusion it seemed as though Irene were surrounded by a sea of serenity as she smiled brightly and ushered them in.

"Come in, gentlemen," she said in a warm, smiling welcome as though their visit were an every-morning occasion. "Can I get you a cup of coffee?"

Matt, in contrast, was an animated picture of impatience. His eyes were dark and stormy as he glanced around until his gaze came to rest on Rocky.

"We didn't come here for coffee," he snarled. "I've come to get my dog!" As he punctuated his words with his hands his stature seemed to take on Paul Bunyan proportions, as one rebellious wisp of hair escaped from his widow's peak. "The sheriff has seen all of my papers and he knows that's my dog," he said, pointing at Rocky, "so just hand him over and we'll get out of here."

"God darn it, boy!" The sheriff bellowed in impatience at Matt. "Now you had just better get yourself under control or I'm going to have to cool your heels a little. This is an investigation and nothing more until I find out exactly what's going on here."

The sheriff was a robust middle-aged man, wiry with rugged features and a booming deep voice. He looked at

Irene kindly, toying with the hat in his hand, obviously embarrassed by Matt's behavior.

"Seems," he said, addressing her in much softer tones, "Mr. Davis feels there is some dispute as to who's the owner of this dog."

The sheriff's eyes had traveled to Rocky. They narrowed perceptibly as he moved closer to the dog and astutely examined the animal's ears. His face hardened as he noted the scratches on the dog's snout. He looked from Irene to Matt. His hand went to the lower profile of his face and he rested his gaze speculatively on Matt.

"You say this dog is yours? What are you planning to do with him?" he asked pointedly.

Seeing the sheriff's concern, all of Irene's original suspicions about Matt returned. A steely control came over her as she resolved to stay calm and stand her ground.

"What do you mean?" asked Matt, obviously annoyed at the sheriff's attitude.

"Well, this dog looks like a pretty good dog—like maybe someone's got some special plans for him," the sheriff said, pointing to Rocky's ears.

"Well, I do," said Matt. Realizing that his impatience and hostility were not helping him, he was making a concerted effort to answer calmly and patiently. "He's an investment and a hobby for me," he continued. "I'm planning to show him in the novice class of the UKC dog show coming in August. It's the only registry that recognizes American pit bull terriers as a breed."

"UK what?" asked the sheriff, scowling, obviously annoyed.

"United Kennel Club," said Irene, breaking in calmly. She looked at Matt, appraising him for a moment, as her eyes met his in an icy stare. "That's the equivalent of our AKC, or American Kennel Club, in Britain, I think, but I didn't know they had a show scheduled for this area."

"Well, they do," said Matt, quietly matching her in composure. He pulled a sheaf of papers from his pocket. "Here's the catalog," he said, handing it to her, "and it's not necessarily British. It's just another purebred dog registry." Their fingers brushed accidentally and an involuntary tremor went through her. Irene was once again aware of his almost overpowering masculinity.

"Let me see that," said the sheriff. Irene handed the catalog to him and he leafed through it hurriedly. "Well, I guess maybe there could be something to what you say, I don't know." He turned to address Irene. "Now this fella, Mr. Davis here, has got all kinds of pedigree papers, and such that says he's the owner of this dog or one just like him. From what he's already told me, he came out here last night and got into it with you over who owns him. So I'd appreciate it, Miss Malone, if you would just tell me how you come to have this animal and what your claim of ownership is."

"Well, it's very simple," said Irene, in a cool, confident voice. "Mr. Davis probably did own a dog like Rocky once and he apparently lost him. But Rocky is mine. He has tags and license to prove it," she said, pointing to the heavy collar that now encircled the dog's massive neck. "Those papers don't have a picture or anything that conclusively identifies Rocky as his." Hearing his name, Rocky came over to nuzzle and playfully tug at Irene's hand. Looking at Matt, her eyes narrowed in determination. "I'm very attached to him and have no intention of giving him up to someone like Mr. Davis."

Tapping the papers in his hand, the sheriff mused to himself, looking first to Matt and then to Irene. Glancing once more at the dog, he took a deep breath and then addressed Matt. "Well, sir, Mr. Davis, I think Miss Malone here has a point. This is a case of your word against hers. We've got laws about dogs having licenses—looks like this dog is registered to her."

"Why, that's just ridiculous!" Matt exploded, losing his hard-won composure completely. "I didn't even lose him until day before yesterday! What are you trying to pull? I paid two hundred and fifty dollars for that dog and he's mine!"

Hearing Matt's voice raised in anger, Rocky had become very quiet. Now he began to growl and whine. Buffy instinctively cowered away from the larger dog that had, only moments before, been his playmate.

"Well, it certainly doesn't look as though you've treated him very well," said Irene, noting the unusual behavior of the dogs. "Sounds like he's been yelled at a lot."

"You don't know what you're talking about," said Matt, so angry now his fists were clenched.

The sheriff stepped toward Matt, placing his hand on his chest. "Cool it, fella," he said authoritatively, "I got no reason to doubt Miss Malone's word. I don't know you from a hill of beans, never seen you around here before, so I think it's best that this dog just stay here for the time being."

Seeing Matt's justified fury, a few pangs of guilt over her acquisition of the animal began to prick Irene's icy composure. Glancing again at the UKC catalog, she could sympathize with Matt if, in fact, he was innocent and her suspicion of his intention to fight Rocky were wrong. People who got involved with these shows usually took them very seriously, putting a lot of time, money, and effort into them. Then she looked down at Rocky and once again saw his ears and those telltale scratches on his snout. No, she just couldn't take the chance. The thought of Rocky in the dogfight pit was too much, but her conscience made her feel bad for Matt just the same.

"Sheriff," she said softly as he began to herd Matt out

the door, "I . . . I don't mean, well . . . I don't want to see Mr. Davis get into any trouble." She continued to stammer, realizing she sounded a little foolish. "I understand how he feels, I really do."

"Save it, lady!" Matt interrupted with a sneer. The plaid of his shirt came alive as his arms moved in anger, giving his face a demonic cast. "You can take your innocent little speeches and shove them. You have got to be the most calculating witch I've ever seen. You deliberately stole my dog!"

All of Irene's anger from the night before returned and a field of angry electric emotions immediately enveloped the two of them. Her words were jagged with fire and her eyes were beams of destruction.

"You beast," she said with disgust, "you haven't got the slightest notion of what's right for that dog. All you can think about is the money you want to make with him—he means nothing to you!"

"Hold it! Hold it!" said the sheriff, stepping between them.

"Get him out of my house," Irene said in cold fury.

"We're leaving," said the sheriff. "I'm sorry for all the commotion."

Pulling his hat firmly over his dark hair, Matt's eyes flashed over Irene in fiery anger, taking in every detail of her trim, taut figure, all the more accentuated by the tight jeans and heaving blouse, as she stood, hands on hips, once again ordering him out. His face was a mask of cold, determined fury. "This isn't over yet," he said as he stomped through the door. "You can just bet that this isn't over yet!"

"Jerk!" cried Irene as the door slammed behind him.

"Again, I'm sorry, Miss Malone," said the sheriff, voicing genuine concern as he put on his hat and reopened the door quietly. "I'll see to it that he doesn't bother you again."

The moment they were gone Irene's arrogant composure crumbled. She fell to the couch and quiet tears began to course down her smooth cheeks. She heard Matt's tires spitting gravel as they tore angrily from her drive. She touched the fingers that had brushed his to the tears on her face. She could feel the whisper of some of her old emotional tormentors as pangs of rejection and regret nudged away her anger, replacing it with a perplexing confusion.

"Rats," she said defiantly. "It's over. He's just another no good man and you're a fool to let him bother you. You're right. You know you are. Now forget it."

Suddenly a great white head was urgently and insistently nudging her as a big moist, pink tongue took a swipe across her face. Buffy's golden body hurtled in to join the fun.

"Rocky, Buffy, you fools," she said as she pushed them away and began to laugh. "Leave me alone." Getting to her feet she dried her tears and lifted her chin in determination. "Come on, guys," she said as the two dogs scampered about her. "We've got work to do. When we get done maybe we'll go to the beach this afternoon."

"Come back here, you two!" The wind whipped the words away, and as Irene's hair blew in front of her, giving her the appearance of walking backward, she knew the dogs never heard her. Using her full arm she fought to sweep her hair back and turned to face the wind so she could see which of the big dunes strewn with sea oats they were disappearing behind. They were two mismatched, oversized puppies completely enthralled with each other. The day had turned a little nippy and cloudy. When she saw she had the beach all to herself she had unleashed the pups. They went tearing down the waterline playfully growling and tugging at one another.

Actually Buffy, with his golden hair flying, was the agitator, flying in and around Rocky, trying desperately to grab him, while Rocky effortlessly shook him off as he loped full speed ahead. He paused every now and then to fall to the sand in a full-scale tussle with the smaller, more agile dog. Then he mouthed him gently and playfully, contrary to the very real nips Buffy's small sharp teeth made on him.

Shoving her hands into her Windbreaker as it ballooned around her body, Irene looked out toward the water, majestic and glorious as its waves, turned to winter gray, rolled in toward her. The last remnants of frothing white caps played around the feet of the busy little seabirds that skittered all over the place scavenging constantly for food. She loved their different shapes and sizes, most of them gray, black, and white, but except for the obvious sea gulls she had trouble telling them apart and remembering what they were.

The beach echoed and magnified her churning emotions as she walked along, watching the dogs from the corner of her eye while thinking about Matt Davis and the events of the past twenty-four hours. She couldn't forget his eyes, and in spite of her animosity she wondered what shape his lips would have if he were to ever really smile.

She felt the nipples of her breasts grow taut, titillated by the caress of the breeze, as she floated unconsciously into a daydream perfectly accompanied by the sea and wind. For a few glorious seconds she remembered the touch of his fingers and the strength of his chest. She looked out to the sea, searching, seeing nothing but the vast heaving expanse of water, and she knew she was lonely. Then, like a wave crashing from a smooth, gentle arc, her dreamy reverie was shattered when she remembered the sneering anger of his voice that morning.

She could feel her own anger returning accompanied by an insidious background rage that seemed to whisper over and over again, "Why?" Why was she suddenly mixed up in something so rotten and degenerate? Why was someone like Matt Davis doing something so terrible, or *was that,* Irene asked herself harshly, *what made him so attractive?* He was exactly the kind of man who would fight dogs, with his big truck and macho overbearing attitude. *Was she,* she continued to query, *one of those sickies who constantly flailed themselves with bad men?*

And yet, something wasn't right. For a few seconds Irene had felt that Matt actually did have a genuine concern for Rocky and maybe, after all, she had overreacted and jumped to some pretty hysterical conclusions. After all, the UKC show was coming next summer and she had, herself, at one time, considered the dog show circuit until she realized what a tough time she would have selling the puppies, which was the real bread and butter in those types of endeavors.

But then why, Irene recalled, did the sheriff readily uphold her ownership of Rocky, making no attempt to reason with her in the face of Matt Davis's proof of ownership? He obviously did not want Davis to have the dog back and *there could be only one reason for that,* she thought sternly, as all of her original suspicions returned.

Kicking her foot into the packed sand, she set her chin and looked about in defiance, trying to catch a glimpse of the dogs.

"Well, forewarned is forearmed," she said resignedly, speaking aloud into the wind. "There's really no need to ever see Matt Davis again, anyway."

Her voice carried to the dogs and they came scampering in, bounding around her feet, barely winded from all of their exercise. As she knelt down they wriggled and fought to shower her with canine affection. Laughing joyously and glad for the release it gave her, she tumbled with them to the sand, trying unsuccessfully to avoid their wet tongues.

"Oh, you guys," she said as she pulled them both close to her, trying to calm their wiggling bodies. Her hands reached out and attempted to encircle Rocky's wide face. He always seemed to have a harried, bewildered, sad expression on his face.

"You really are ugly," she said to him fondly. "I don't think I've ever seen an uglier head and yet, my God, you're beautiful. Your spirit is wonderful, and . . ." she continued, her fingers tracing the lines of his great mouth, "you're so sweet and gentle . . . I just can't imagine . . ." Massaging the supple, generous folds of skin around his face she remembered the purpose of his special body conformation and her anger returned.

What had he said when he stomped out that morning? Flashing back, Matt Davis's angry words echoed in her mind. "You can just bet that this isn't over yet!"

What if he decided to take her to court? Remembering again how she had actually acquired Rocky, Irene felt a twinge of panic. Or worse yet, what if he simply stole him? After all, he did have the registration papers and . . .

She realized she was being carried away again by irrational emotions obviously the result of the guilt she couldn't seem to shake over her decision to keep the dog. "Really," she admonished herself impatiently, "you've got to stop reacting like a guilty schoolgirl. You are letting your imagination get completely out of hand."

Sighing, she looked at her watch and realized the clouds would soon be turning to darkness. Calling the dogs, she lifted her head and met the wind, matching its strength with her own. She had done the right thing. As Rocky raced ahead toward the car she could feel her heart bounding with him and she knew she must do everything in her power to protect him.

Looking toward the sky, which seemed to swirl about her, she involuntarily tossed out a quick prayer, seeking forgiveness for her transgression, if in fact she had committed one. Innately she somehow knew that Matt Davis was a man of his word and this wasn't over yet. As she walked on she could feel again a deep warmth beginning to radiate throughout her body; something instinctive, primitive, and expectant as she thought again of flashing dark eyes and sensuous lips, something that, indeed, agreed this wasn't over yet.

Later in the evening Irene walked lightly around the chalet in her usual end-of-the-day routine. Her trip to the beach had refreshed and invigorated her. Evening chores had been a breeze. Now she was relaxed, ready for bed. As she straightened and picked up just enough to assure herself of some semblance of order her silky robe swished about her, accompanied by soft symphonic music, giving her movements the elegance of a ballerina performing a household commercial on TV. When her arms reached gracefully overhead to snap out the dim dining-area light the illusion was complete, only to be dispelled instantaneously as she clicked the stereo off and continued on into the sanctuary of her bedroom with its comfortable, elegant furnishings, completely in sync with the rustic charm of the house.

She had accomplished this by blending the simplicity and elegance of Danish lines in her bed and bureau with the comfort of a large early American wing chair and ottoman, upholstered in warm velvet in the cooler months and, with a flip and snap of the coverings, a cool print when the weather warmed up. A handmade afghan in a modern design lay folded over its back. A special custom-

37

made modern quilt carefully integrated with a traditional pattern from the past, the Star of David, covered the bed and completed the effect, mirrored in floor-to-ceiling windows that looked out on her deck and the forest behind.

She walked lightly to the drapes and closed them, instantly transforming the room into a comfortable, private abode lighted only by the small elegant light on the nightstand.

Irene had chosen the furnishings of her home very carefully, adamant about having exactly what she wanted for both comfort and beauty, chintzing on nothing as a tribute to her sense of self-esteem. For the same reason she always slept in elegant nightgowns and relaxed in colorful caftans or simple long, loose-fitting cotton dresses in exotic prints. Her bed was made with the finest linens in bright coordinated prints. She had an abundance of thick, luxurious towels, and the carpet throughout her home whispered a caress of understated refinement and comfort with every step she took.

As she began to remove the bedspread she reminded herself that she deserved these things. It was one of the most therapeutic realizations she had made in her quest for independence and self-fulfillment after the divorce. She had felt a great sense of satisfaction as she acquired them in careful accordance with her overall objectives of realistic, permanent financial security.

Recently, though, she had begun to realize that her life was beginning to feel a little empty. Oh, certainly, she had friends and often enjoyed and shared activities with them. She especially enjoyed hostessing small dinners and was surprised to find that she had soon established a well-rounded group of acquaintances who enjoyed good books and wine, who readily engaged in sophisticated, philosophical discussions when the mood was right. It was a paradox found in so many small vacation communities that had suddenly been discovered by the weary refugees of big-city stress. Some people actually commuted by jet, but the majority, of course, were still the descendants of the original inhabitants and, while throughly modern in many ways, still clung to the close-knit ways of a back-woods community. Irene liked the contrast, though, and was appreciative of the fact that she found it easy to interact in both realms. To be sure, there was ignorance and closed minds in both circles, but on the whole her life was very interesting and complete—that is, that is what she had thought until she had experienced this unexpect-ed, abrasive confrontation with this disturbing man, Matt Davis. In spite of her anger and disapproval Irene had to admit to herself that he seemed to have some strange power to elicit an almost primitive and most decidedly inappropriate response from her.

A longing she had tried very carefully to sublimate was now becoming more insistent and she was disturbed that she might, after all, feel a need to establish a relationship just for the purpose of physical release. The thought barely flickered through her mind, however, before Irene dis-counted it, knowing, as always, that for her, satisfaction was only possible when accompanied by an emotional commitment as well. She was, nevertheless, beginning to realize that she missed, even more than not being loved, having someone to love. It was obvious that she needed to begin to search for a productive relationship, compatible with her own mores. She mused, in conclusion, *her body was clearly trying to tell her something.*

Picking up a thick novel from the bedside table, she slid into the refreshing smoothness of her bed. She turned and stacked the pillows and then settled back for the enjoyable relaxation that reading at this time always gave her, al-though it often resulted in her drifting into sleep with the book still in hand. As her hands relaxed they would release the book, which usually slid to the floor with a thud, arousing her momentarily to replace it on the table and turn out the light.

Rocky and Buffy both quickly dropped close to the bed in sentry positions, front paws straight out with muzzles resting on them, ending their close scrutiny of Irene during the past few moments. They had started out this way the night before, Rocky extremely intent, with furrowed face and eyes watching her carefully; but soon both dogs were on their sides in an abandoned sprawl. They barely noticed as Irene groggily turned out the light and settled into the bed. Within moments she was drifting into another world, at first floating and ethereal and then, very real.

She was drawn to a warmth; hard, muscular, solid warmth. She moaned and moved, fitting her body to the curving masculine back. Then she secured herself by tucking her knees into the bent lock of his while folding her arms around his solid torso. Slowly her long fingers began to weave and twine through the erotic curling hair on his hard belly. Her lips silently caressed the smoothness of his shoulder as she willed him to awake slowly and sensuously. Languidly he stirred, murmuring pleasure in his sleep as her hand traveled slowly upward, twirling the thick, dark hair of his chest about the tips of her long fingers as her tapered nails left a titillating track upon his skin. Seductively she moved her legs against the hard muscles of his thighs, awakening yet another area of sensitivity as her entire body began to respond to his. Teasing, her fingers circled the hard flat nipples of his breasts, and she felt them grow taut and rigid in unison with her own. As he turned slightly in delicious grogginess, unconsciously beginning to respond, his hand began to grope, feeling the nakedness of her thigh, while moving to encircle the softness of her pale bottom. His still sleeping head began to roll over her arm seeking the nurture of her breast as her fingers coursed through his hair, pursuing the interesting contours of his ears. Her middle finger stroked the softness of his earlobe while she raised herself to better meet the promise of his lips around her ready breast.

In one motion he enveloped her in his massive strength and turned her beneath him. His hands began to trail the length of her eager body while the succor of her breast wakened him to a commanding arousal. Leisurely his lips traveled over her neck, soft and demanding, until at last they devoured her lips, silencing her murmurs of need as his hard, urgent tongue fenced hers into submission. Submerged completely in warm, instinctive darkness, her body responded, urgently signaling his on as her hand caressed and massaged the hard muscles of his back, arched now, ready to possess her.

Moving her legs slowly, she manuevered to prolong the crescendo of anticipation as his rigid male strength probed urgently, touching the softness of her inner thigh. Slowly and delicately her fingers stroked that strength and the underlying softness as she swung her long leg over his. The full promise of his manhood grew, giving her an exhilarating sense of satisfaction and power laced with tenderness and need, as she softly rolled above him. She began to move in unison with the primitive beat of her instincts while the tips of her breasts touched the nipples of his and her hands, grasping the sides of his head, buried themselves completely in dark, wavy, resilient hair. Her face mirrored the joy of his thrusting momentum as the rigid tip of his love whispered repeatedly over her pulsing button of desire. His strong hands grasped her buttocks, pulled her ever closer to him. She moved in wild abandon, kissing him deeply as she gave in to the invitation she had extended. His strength entered her, deep and pulsating, as he hammered her wildly and gently into ecstasy completely in unison with his own. As his last soft pulses receded,

41

filling her to overflowing, her lips brushed soft eyelids and strong chiseled features, faintly familiar, framed by a widow's peak, as she idly drifted into another mode of slumber, turning peacefully in her bed. As her body continued to drift and float he moved airily away. She felt no sense of pain or panic, but on the contrary a great sense of satisfaction. In abandoned release she sublimely relaxed into deep and fulfilling slumber, tucking the dream sweetly away into her subconscious, only wisps of which she would remember when she arose.

CHAPTER THREE

Walking into the kennel early the next morning, Irene reached for her gum boots as she rolled her jeans up and tightened the ribbon around her hair. In the fickle fashion of the weather in the panhandle the day promised to be very warm. Already it was hot and steamy, so she was looking forward to washing down the runs with the cool pressurized water. Quickly she pulled some large bobby pins from her pockets and deftly twirled her long hair up into a quasi-French knot. Feeling instantly cooler, she reached for the keys to the kennel doors and went in to see her residents, all of whom were overjoyed at her entrance.

Although the winter in Cramdon was usually little more than an occasional nippy nuisance of two or three months duration, when the warming trend in March indicated a hint of permanence most of the young natives disappeared for an almost ritual hiatus at the beach, where the first spring rays of the sun initiated them into another year of vigorous, healthy tans. It was a rather convenient coincidence that her young helper, Jeff, had called in sick this morning. Irene was not in any way deluded but remembered well her own youthful joy during those first heady days that heralded the advent of spring after a long, cold winter. It was easy to excuse a young man who for the most part was reliable.

Basking in her own feelings of benevolence as she reached for a hose, Irene realized wryly that her attitude was in fact rather matronly when one considered that she was only twenty-seven now, not that many years older than Jeff.

"Well, sports," she said resignedly to the yapping dogs all around her, "maybe I am turning into an old lady." Thinking back over the events of the past few days, she continued musingly, "A grouchy old lady at that."

Turning on the hose, she began methodically to hose down each of the runs after carefully moving the inhabitants to the outdoor run and closing them off until the inside was cleaned, sanitized, and squeegeed dry. She would repeat the process on the outside—all in all, a rather tedious and sloppy job unless you liked animals, but Irene honestly enjoyed the physical contact with the dogs. Most of them looked upon the entire process as a big game. This was a chore usually done by Jeff, but she didn't mind doing it once in a while just to keep her hand in. Often it brought some things to her attention, such as the leaky hose she was using now, which somehow had not been mentioned so it could be repaired or replaced.

The leak really was annoying and should have been wrapped with tape long ago. It was located near the nozzle and Irene's thin cotton T-shirt was soon soaked through. It was a big sloppy shirt, so, thinking in terms of comfort, she had elected to go braless that morning. Her appearance was now rapidly beginning to resemble that of a teasing *Playboy* pinup. She discovered that she could control the squirting stream of water by keeping her hand over the hole as she held the nozzle. This was obviously what Jeff had been doing for some time rather than stop and shut everything down to go and look for tape. It irritated Irene, though, that Jeff couldn't have remembered to mention it or fix it after finishing the chores.

In spite of her good intentions her hand frequently slipped or she forgot the leak as she grabbed for the hose and used it in a much practiced, automatic motion. Soon she was completely drenched. She was alone, though, and in the steamy room it felt good so she decided to finish and then go in and change before opening to the public.

She was completely immersed in her work, squeegeeing the floors dry, when she heard the bell announcing that the front kennel door in the lobby had opened.

"Oh, my gosh!" she panicked. Had she left the front door open? She looked around for something to cover herself and found nothing. One of the first rules of a well-run, clean kennel was that nothing extraneous be left around to catch dirt or breed infection. The gleaming walls and stainless steel winked back at her in mockery.

"Anybody home?" a deep voice called from the lobby. Irene's heart stopped for a second as she gasped. She could feel herself growing warm all over as she crossed her arms protectively over her sodden breasts, which were outlined nakedly through her drenched shirt. It hung sloppily and heavily about her, clinging to and accentuating the generous curves above her tight jeans.

It was him—the stranger, Matt Davis. Irene would never forget that voice after yesterday. What was he doing here? The sheriff had told him to stay away. What did he want? Curiously, his voice sounded friendly.

Looking around furtively, trying not to panic, she spotted a large towel she had just used to dry the long hair of a big collie that had insisted on playing with the water as it streamed from the hose. Grabbing it, she called out.

"Just a minute. I'll be there in just a minute." Her hands were trembling as she tried frantically to secure the towel around her. She wrapped it tightly and fastened it by stuffing a corner in beneath her arm, which she then firmly clamped down.

Had he come back to try and get Rocky again? Dazedly Irene tried to remember if she had let the dog out or if he was still in the house with Buffy. "Oh, I've been careless!" she admonished herself. What was to stop him from just grabbing the dog—in the kennel she wouldn't have heard him. She could feel her blood rising as she thought, *I wouldn't put it past him to come in here and tell me in his own snide, cynical way that he was grabbing him in broad daylight—daring me to do anything about it!*"

The momentum of her panic and anger sent her barreling through the door, but as she fastened the towel a little more securely she willed herself to speak calmly, an exercise that demanded every ounce of her inner strength.

"I'm sorry, the kennel isn't open until ten."

"Seems like I've heard that before," he said genially. He was leaning on the counter, hat in hand. A smile crinkled his features, giving him the appearance of an old-time cowboy hero about to address a frail, feminine damsel in distress.

Irene's appearance did little to dispel the intent. As she came through the door her eyes were wide and darting. Damp tendrils of her long hair hung lankly about her face as she clutched the towel about her. She could have easily fulfilled the role of a cold and hungry waif trudging the streets of a rainy London dock reminiscent of Dickens' tragic children, had not the force of her words betrayed a spirit completely in stride with modern maturity.

"What are you doing here?" she questioned haughtily. "I thought the sheriff made it clear that you were to stay away from here."

"W-a-a-ait a minute," Matt drawled out placatingly as he reached around to his hind pocket and drew out a snowy white handkerchief. "Truce," he said as he waved it and continued to grin at her. "I come in peace," he continued, motioning with his palms up as the handkerchief continued to flutter from his thumb and index finger. "I just want to talk and see if we can't come to some amicable agreement."

"I understood that this matter was settled yesterday," Irene said pointedly. "There is nothing to discuss."

As she talked she could feel his eyes wandering over her, warm, friendly, and amused. She looked away, unable to meet his eyes, and grew warmly uncomfortable as she realized how she must look. Just the thought of his nearness was unsettling enough, but the reality was almost unbearable. She cursed herself for reacting in such a sophomoric way.

"Really, I'm not going to change my mind," she continued rapidly. "Rocky is mine and I intend to keep him. There is nothing that we can possibly discuss that would, in any way, be productive." Irene had chosen her words carefully and delivered them in a prim, decisive way in an effort to exhibit her strength and intelligence. "Now I really *must* get back to work. I'm all alone today and, as you can readily see, I am not ready to greet the public."

As she turned sharply to leave him the corner of the counter caught the edge of her protective towel and it tumbled swiftly and heavily about her feet, having absorbed a great deal of moisture from her wet clothes. She gasped and quickly turned away from him but not before Matt had taken in her obvious state of undress. Mortified, but suddenly sick of this whole schoolgirl charade, she instantly realized that her old ally, her sense of humor, was the only thing that could in any way extricate her from this situation with some semblance of grace.

"Well," Irene said as she quickly swooped the towel up. A mischievous glint lit up her face as she laughingly went on. "I seem to be forever and a day finding myself undressed or half-naked in your presence." She looked him straight in the eye and was pleased to note a hint of discomfiture as she languidly rewrapped the towel, not caring at all if he watched. His eyes followed her nimble fingers in hypnotic fascination as in the few seconds before she once again secured the towel beneath her arm, the outline of her taut nipples and firm breasts peeked tantalizingly through the thin, opaque film of the now partially dry shirt accompanied by her rapid breathing.

"My pleasure, indeed," he responded as he continued to watch her movements and made no effort to subdue a teasing smile.

Cad, she seethed to herself. He would not one-up her! She had nothing to hide. After all, anyone brave enough could go braless on the beach if they wanted to. She was on her own property and her appearance was completely justified. Why should she let this bother her?

"I wouldn't want you getting any wrong ideas," she stated matter-of-factly. "I've got a leak in the hose and I just didn't have time to fix it."

"Not at all," he said magnanimously. "As a matter of fact," he said, giving her a mischievous wink, "I'd be more than glad to come back and give you a hand if that hose can make you look the way I think it can."

"You cad," Irene said out loud this time, but she found herself laughing in spite of herself. Her anger had somehow simply and mysteriously disappeared and she was warmly responding to his banter.

"Seriously," Matt said, seeing the change in her mood, "I did come out just to talk to you this morning and . . . well . . . to apologize." He spoke thoughtfully, but authoritatively. "I think," he went on rapidly, "we got off on the wrong foot right from the beginning and this whole thing is just one giant exercise in misunderstanding."

Seeing Irene begin to bristle again, he went on quickly to reassure her. "Don't get me wrong. I didn't come here to talk about taking Rocky away—that is what you call him, isn't it?" he queried, pausing momentarily.

Irene nodded absently as she watched him intently, puzzled and surprised by this change in his attitude. Somehow this seemed more treacherous than when he was angry, and she felt an instinctive distrust of what he was about to say.

"Anyway," Matt continued, "seeing the kind of setup you have here, I think maybe the sheriff is right. The dog probably is better off here. I'm working with a local construction company and just staying in a small motel until I can get settled, which isn't the best place to keep a dog, especially one like Rocky, so I'm hoping maybe we can go back to square one and start all over again."

Glancing at the clock, Irene saw that she had very little time left until the kennel opened to the public. "That's all well and good," she said politely, "but I've got a kennel that needs to have the cleaning finished before I open to the public, so maybe we'd better discuss this some other time."

"Seriously, let me give you a hand," he offered affably. "There's not much to do around here on a Saturday—the beaches are a madhouse, full of kids today. Then maybe we can talk later."

"Really, that's not necessary," she said, once again aware of his masculinity as her eyes met his. Her heart began to beat rapidly, but her outward veneer of calm effectively concealed her inner battle to control her rampant response to him.

"I *want* to help you," he said in exasperation that hinted

at a touch of annoyance. "It's no trouble and I do know a good deal about animals."

Looking at the clock once more, which had continued to tick relentlessly on, Irene decided she really did need some help now to open on time. Against her better judgment she made an instantaneous about-face, as she relented and motioned for him to follow her. "Let's get with it, then. I've still got a lot to do."

Matt quickly shed his shirt, baring his massive chest and well-developed arms, as he followed her with a roguish grin.

Again, Irene steeled herself to the sophomoric response that his physique always seemed to evoke from her. She was dizzied by her awareness as his magnetism radiated about her, mingling compatibly with the other animal vibrations in the room and all the more intensified by his crafty, innocent jocularity. Quickly grabbing a smock from the lobby closet, she marched straight ahead as she put it on. She was grateful for the camouflage it provided both physically and emotionally. Seconds later the cool water of the hose had returned her to some aspect of normality.

Within moments they were both involved in the work. As Matt fed the dogs while Irene attended to the cats, she had to admit that he had a way with animals. They had taken to him quickly, responding readily to his instinctive confidence as he handled them firmly but gently. He chattered with them amicably and seemed to be well-acquainted with kennel procedure.

"I told you I'd had a lot of experience with animals," Matt responded to her rather quizzical appraisal of him as they sat down for a moment to catch their breath. Irene was sipping a can of cold juice and had wordlessly offered him one, making no attempt to mask her puzzlement. He sat back with a sigh and chugalugged most of the can.

Using his T-shirt, he ruffled his damp hair into tousled chaos before deftly pulling it over his torso in a practiced motion. He relaxed again in a disjointed sprawl and looked at her, grinning warmly. "You've really got a great operation here."

There was obvious respect in his voice, and Irene could feel herself growing uncomfortable again as a pulse began to throb in her throat.

"Yes, I guess so," she responded. "I try to do my best." She once again glanced at the clock to avoid meeting his gaze. "But right now, I've got to run in and change. It's almost time to open." Feeling self-conscious, she made an attempt to thank him and dismiss him at the same time. "Listen, I really do appreciate your help, but I think I can manage now."

In spite of his obviously sincere care and concern for the animals, Irene was having second thoughts as her insidious suspicions began to surface again. One thing a successful dogfighter had to be was a superb handler of animals. Another of the ironies of that sickening business was that the animals fought at the bidding of their handlers. Their owners often identified with them and extolled the virtues of dogs that fought for them in spite of grievous injuries. A truly "game" or brave dog needed the expertise of a knowledgeable handler to survive the pit and, more importantly, not disgrace his owner by turning and running when it instinctively knew it was beaten. The latter animals were labled "curs" and usually destroyed.

Irene shuddered as she glanced again at Matt, who had made no move to leave, and recalled how she had gained much of her knowledge about this activity. She had often heard people discussing it openly in the general store, which also served as the town gathering spot, when she had occasion to visit Cedarville, the town nestled in the pine forest north of Cramdon.

51

She gave a start as a warm hand came down on her shoulder, bringing her out of the reverie she had drifted into unconsciously.

"Hey there," Matt said, grinning, "you haven't heard a word I've said."

"Oh, I'm sorry," she said, a little flustered. "I was just thinking about something."

She realized that she still had not gone in to change and now it was too late. David Thornton's sleek car pulled up in the drive. She felt Matt grow tense as the handsome man stepped out of his car, smoothed his mustache, and headed for the door.

"Hi there, Irene," David said warmly and exuberantly. "I hear you've gotten yourself a pit bull."

She was stunned. There were obviously no secrets in this place. She knew it was a small community, but this was ridiculous.

"How on earth did you learn about that?" Irene asked, obviously annoyed.

"Oh, don't you worry your pretty head about that," he said, laughing. Looking around, he continued, "Where is it, I hear . . ." He stopped in midsentence as he became aware of Matt's presence.

Regaining her composure, Irene looked from one man to the other and then began to hastily introduce them. David was a prominent, well-to-do country lawyer from Cedarville who was known in the area as a breeder of pit bulls. Matt's demeanor from the previous day seemed to have returned.

"The dog you are referring to," Matt said firmly, "happens to be mine. Miss Malone and I had a little misunderstanding about him, but we've worked that out. She's been kind enough to offer to keep him here while I'm getting him ready for the UKC show coming up next summer."

Irene looked at Matt in total disbelief. *The nerve of him,* she thought, but she watched silently as, to her amazement, the lawyer looked at Matt knowingly and extended his hand in greeting.

"Yours in the sport," David said meaningfully.

Matt hesitated momentarily. His gaze seemed to shift, almost imperceptibly calculating and wary as he groped for words. "Sure. . . . Right on," he said in return as he met the other man's hand in a firm shake.

For a moment Irene felt as if she were in a cheap spy novel. Then suddenly David glanced at his watch and feigned a businesslike alarm.

"Going to have to run," he said as he gave Irene a quick squeeze that was a little more familiarity than she cared for. Again she sensed Matt's eyes, hard and probing. "I only had a minute before I had to get to court, but I heard about your dog and couldn't wait to see him. I guess I'll have to catch you later." Irene nodded mutely as David turned and went out the door, calling good-byes as he went.

All of the earlier rapport established between them had vanished as Irene turned savagely to address Matt, who had stepped to the window to watch David pull away.

"How dare you," she began, but he seemed oblivious to her. She could feel his tension as he finally turned and recognized her. He was obviously preoccupied, immersed in his own thoughts, but he made an effort to appease her.

"Look, I know that was a little out of line, but that's what I came out to talk to you about. I really did sink a lot of money into that dog and I'd really like to have the chance to show him. On the other hand I could never afford a place like this for him so I thought maybe we could sit down like two sensible adults and work this thing out."

"You're assuming an awful lot, aren't you? What makes

you think I am about to acknowledge any claim you think you have?"

"Look, I'm not challenging you," he said. "I don't want to get into all of that again, but you and I both know the score. All I'm asking you to do is let me visit and work out with him. Get to know me a little better. After all, the registration-pedigree papers are in my name. What's wrong with wanting to show a dog in a dog show?"

In spite of herself Irene found herself responding to Matt's sincerity. Maybe she was overreacting. In final analysis her judgment was based solely on her own assumptions. She had no substantial proof of any kind that he was anything other than what he claimed to be. His explanations were ultimately reasonable when considered objectively. She looked at him for several moments, trying to decide how to respond. His gaze never left her and once again she could feel herself beginning to blush.

"Well, I guess it wouldn't do any harm, but you've got to promise to come only when I'm here—and I want to know what the exact requirements of that show are," she finished firmly.

"Yes, ma'am," he said genially, once again breaking into a grin.

Irene laughed too, grateful that the tension seemed to ease.

"You see your friend often?" Matt asked casually, changing the subject completely. Irene sensed a note of falseness in his voice.

Once again her emotions clouded as she remembered that David had greeted Matt knowingly and conspiratorially. "Yours in the sport" was a common salutation among dogfighters. For that matter, it was a little shocking to have heard David use it too, although Irene had to admit she had heard talk. Was she in her silliness knowingly putting Rocky in danger? She still had reason to believe that Matt wasn't above using her or the dog for his ultimate ends. Deciding it was time to settle this once and for all, she spoke deliberately.

"You know, of course, that illegal underground dogfighting is a big sport around here, don't you?" She stepped back to gauge his reaction. "And Rocky is the breed of dog most often used." Perceptively she saw the corner of his eye give a little twitch as he looked at her with a stony, unperturbed face. The moment was a treacherous one and the silence hung between them, a taut string that both refused to break.

Matt stood in a wide-legged stance, arms crossed, watching her carefully. "Oh, sure," he said, finally shattering the deathly stillness. "You hear talk all the time, especially up around Cedarville. From what I hear, though, the sheriff around here is pretty tough, but doesn't get much help." Checking her response, he ran his hands through his still-tousled hair. "Too bad, too—the pit bull makes a great family pet, from what I've learned from the UKC. It would be a shame to see Rocky used in such a way."

"Oh, it would, would it?" Irene was not about to be taken in by this suddenly boyish, innocent sincerity.

"Yes, to be truthful," he said, continuing to fence with her in double innuendos, "I'm surprised to see that you have such an interest in this breed of dog."

He had turned the tables on her, leaving her on the defensive, which was the last thing Irene had expected. She was angry again. "The truth is," she said, looking at him meaningfully, "this terrible 'sport' flourishes because of people whose only interest is the money involved, upstarts who think they can make a killing by getting a dog and throwing him into the pit, never caring what happens to the animal."

Once again they stared at each other in uneasy silence.

Irene was now definitely having second thoughts about their continued relationship and was just about to inform him that she had changed her mind about his coming to work with Rocky when she heard a powerful pickup truck pull into the drive next to the kennel. In surprise she realized it was his, and an attractive blonde, who at first glance reminded Irene of a Kewpie doll, was behind the wheel.

"Oh, that must be Lola," Matt said in obvious relief as he gathered up his things. "She must have gotten her shopping done."

Irene instantly felt like a fool. "You must have been pretty confident that you . . ."

"Now don't get your dander up again," he said teasingly, the conversation of a moment ago apparently forgotten. He came over and casually lifted her chin with his forefinger and forced her to meet his eyes. "I walked out here this morning. It was such a wonderful day, I thought even if you threw me out, the walk would be worth it." Gesturing toward the truck, he continued. "Lola's probably wondering what happened to me."

Irene looked at him silently. A twinge of distrust and—she hated to admit it—jealousy seared her stomach. Matt started through the door as the other woman opened the door of the truck to get out. Their eyes met in some affirmative communication. Irene noted that the woman was clad in a very suggestive gauzy blouse over tight jeans and stylish boots.

In confusion Irene tried once again to avoid Matt's gaze as he stepped back inside. He turned her slowly toward him and held her firmly by the shoulders. All amusement and teasing were gone as he looked at her very intently, searching her face. He looked past her to the blonde, who was waiting patiently, and then toward the house, where Rocky was sleeping on the deck. For just a second Irene saw genuine concern in his eyes. He took a deep breath and slowly expelled it as he obviously wrestled with his feelings versus his better judgment.

"I know what you are thinking," he said as he looked at her probingly, appealing to her. "It's not what you think," he said huskily as he continued to look at her deeply. "Believe me, this whole thing is not what you think."

In a stunned rare second of insight Irene sensed the presence of truth, but she could not identify its proper application as she returned his gaze.

Quickly, before she could speak, he released her and went through the door. She stared after him in total confusion.

CHAPTER FOUR

"Here I am, just like we agreed!"

In all of your charming, brazen, snide glory, Irene thought cynically to herself as she met Matt's teasing eyes.

She had just left the kennel after a lazy Sunday morning and she was looking forward to a few hours in the sun. She wasn't expecting any new arrivals or pickups at the kennel until later in the day. She had heard the big wheels of his truck long before he appeared and she steeled herself to take care of an unpleasant task. After careful analysis, common sense had told her that this relationship that he had proposed yesterday was not in her or Rocky's best interests. She proposed to so inform him now.

"Look, I've been thinking this over . . ." she began.

"And you're wondering just who this guy is who's coming around and stirring everything up," Matt broke in, grinning at her mischievously.

Unlike the two previous nights, Irene had not slept well the night before and it had left her feeling tired and irritable. She couldn't seem to rid herself of this compelling sense of confusion, which, combined with her genuine concern for Rocky and her overwhelming response to this stranger, was becoming a very real threat to her hard-won, peaceful existence.

"No, really," she said, "I think we need to seriously reexamine this." She had purposely taken on her role as a polished businesswoman, making a real effort to inject a note of condescension in her voice. Today she was going to act like an adult and put these schoolgirl responses behind her.

"I really don't think it is in either of our best interests to continue with this charade."

Irene kept remembering his parting words from the day before: "This whole thing is not what you think." They echoed constantly through her mind, a sly taunting whisper in her deep subconscious.

"I don't know exactly what your game is," she went on, "but I do know that I have no intention of giving Rocky up and there is no need to prolong this."

"My, my, my, aren't we touchy today?" His voice was teasing and companionable, but perhaps a bit too familiar. "I thought we had this all settled. You must know by now that I am not a boogeyman and I have every reason in the world to want that dog to stay here." His eyes danced over her merrily. He was seemingly impervious to her resolve, ignoring everything she was trying to say. "Now what do you say we just settle this once and for all. I think I'm being more than reasonable under the circumstances." Almost imperceptibly he had become quite serious and the tone of his voice took on a menacing note.

Irene struggled to overcome a twinge of panic that fluttered in her stomach.

"You know, of course," he went on, "that I could probably overturn the sheriff's ruling in this matter if I wanted to push it. . . ."

For a moment the silence between them was unreal, still

and laden with tension as he paused speculatively. "But then," he said, breaking in expansively when she remained silent, "what good would that do? Then I'd have to find a place for Rocky to stay and you'd hate me and be worried sick at the same time."

His words were coated with undeniable sincerity. His outstretched arms seemed to beckon to her and she felt irresistibly drawn to them. Flushing, she turned away. With a sigh he dropped his arms to his sides and the moment lightened.

"There isn't any reason why we can't be friends," he said with a somewhat contrived chuckle. "You don't know it, but we've really got a lot in common."

Feeling beaten, Irene realized there was something to what he said. She should probably just make the best of an awkward situation. At least she was assured that the dog would stay in her custody under her control. "I guess maybe you have a point," she said reluctantly.

"Good!" he said enthusiastically. "I knew you would see it my way. Now, if it's all right with you, do you mind if I get reacquainted with my dog?"

"No, of course not," she stammered. "I was just planning to soak up some sun. . . ."

"Well, don't let me bother you," he said with a lascivious wink. "Especially if you're planning on wearing a skimpy bikini."

"Maybe I wasn't planning on wearing anything at all," she said snidely, infuriated with his familiarity and arrogance. "But then, *that* is really none of your business, is it?"

"No, ma'am," he said, grinning expansively, ignoring the challenge of her temperament. "As far as I'm concerned you can do whatever your little heart desires. Just act as though I'm not around."

Beast! He had done it again. Outrageous statements

were completely out of character for Irene and it was unspeakably infuriating to have her cynical attempts at worldliness so easily parried, leaving her feeling like an utter fool. Cad that he was, Matt was enjoying every minute of it while she had nothing but her pride to carry her through. Refusing to allow him the satisfaction of seeing her discomfiture she quickly matched his teasing grin. Her eyes flashed at him seductively.

"Indeed," Irene said imperiously, as she turned to enter the house. When she brushed past him, pretentious and haughty, Matt couldn't resist giving her bottom a playful swat.

Stunned, Irene turned on him, an instant banshee. "I don't believe you did that," she blustered in outrage.

"Believe it," he said mischievously. Delighted with her wild-eyed reaction, he made no attempt to control his glee as she scampered, seething, away.

Moments later Irene was still trying to calm down as she inspected the blush that enshrouded her entire body. That swat had set off a sensuous reaction so shattering that, had she not been alone in the privacy of her bedroom, she would have been chagrined beyond words. Tentacles of fire streaked through her as her fingers gently probed the offended spot.

"I can't believe you are letting this happen to you," she said out loud. Whispers of pleasure from another time seemed to tease her, adding to her confusion. "I think it is time to be adult and realistic about this," she continued. "You can't do anything about his coming around so it is up to you to get to know him. This is a silly physical infatuation spawned by your need for a real relationship. As you get better acquainted, reality will take the place of fantasy. His detractions and faults will become quite obvious, and poof, that will be the end of the attraction."

That is what all of the books and psychologists said.

This was a simple, physical rebound syndrome common to most women in her situation. She was armed. She had educated herself during the transition period that followed the divorce. She could handle it. Having settled that in her mind, she felt immediately comforted.

Quickly she donned her most conservative bikini and headed for the lounge on her deck. When she went out Matt and Rocky were nowhere to be seen. Involuntarily she felt an immediate twinge of panic, but she squelched it quickly, realizing how illogical it was. As she settled down the warm rays of the sun soon lulled her into a restful sleep, compensating for her loss from the night before.

"Hey, sleepyhead." Matt was covering her with one of the afghans from the screened porch. "By golly, you did just about decide to go without clothes, didn't you?" The amusement in his eyes was gentle and Irene found herself responding to it warmly. The sun had suddenly disappeared and the air had taken on a distinct chill.

"What time is it?" she asked, somewhat bewildered.

"Oh, it's going on three or so."

"Oh, my gosh," she said as she began to get up hastily.

"No need to worry," Matt said companionably, "I took care of your pickups from the kennel. Nothing to it. You've got everything pretty well worked out. You seemed so grouchy this morning that I thought it best to just leave you to your nap."

Irene blinked and squinted at him, not quite comprehending what he had just said. "You mean, you took care of my kennel business?" she asked.

Sure thing," he said. "Glad to help out."

"Well . . . then, I guess maybe I should thank you," she said slowly, remembering her resolve earlier in the day. "It's not like me to just doze off like that."

"Seemed more like a coma to me," Matt said, ever mischievous.

If ever a man could epitomize a paradox in mood shifts, this one could, thought Irene. In some ways he resembled the pit bulls, a comedian one minute and a threatening aggressor the next. Not wanting him to guess her thoughts, she made an effort to return his banter, but as she began to move Irene realized that she had been in the sun too long and parts of her were decidedly tender.

"Oh," she groaned as she walked gingerly.

"Here, let me help you," he said, genuinely concerned.

"No, that's okay," she said, not wanting him to touch her when she was so vulnerable, but she was too late. His arm went firmly around her as she hastily grabbed for the skimpy coverup that matched her bikini. She was instantly enfolded in the effusion of his warmth. Instinctively Matt pulled her to him while his lips sought hers sweetly and softly and then gently nuzzled her nose as he brushed her hair back in a soothing caress.

It was an innocent and sweet moment, not demanding in any way and, in fact, perfectly natural. For a second neither of them realized what had happened as they continued to gaze at one another, locked in warmth and gentleness.

"Go on with you," he said huskily, as he broke the silence gently. "I'll get the dogs in and then I thought maybe I could take you to dinner tonight."

"Oh, no," Irene protested weakly, "I'm really not up to it tonight." Shaky and unsettled, this was not exactly what she had had in mind when she formulated her strategy for self-preservation earlier. "I'll share a cup of coffee with you though." She spoke brightly, doing her part to ease them through an awkward, but nevertheless memorably tender moment.

"That's a deal," he said, regaining his earlier exuberance.

"Right," she said, still touched by the moment. Curiously though, she felt no confusion or chagrin. That had been the most incredibly natural caress she had ever experienced, completely without strings, just a mutual expression completely in sync with the moment between two caring people. She felt grateful and warm. "Be with you in just a moment. I think I've been cavorting around like this about long enough." The joke hit home and they both laughed in relief as she left him.

In the sanctuary of her bedroom she quickly pulled on one of her long, loose exotic print dresses and went to rejoin him. The dress was a wonderful reflection of the radiance that now emanated from her naturally. For the first time in days she felt relaxed and comfortable. She stopped in the kitchen to prepare the coffee and found that Matt had already begun it. Contrary to her earlier feelings she felt no irritation over his obvious ability to just make himself at home. Pouring the coffee, she placed it on the tray he had prepared and went out to the screened porch.

When she came through the door, he was unnaturally quiet as he gazed at her, somewhat bewitched. In confusion, he looked away and seemed to search for something appropriate to say. Deftly Irene set the tray down on a redwood table and then nearly stumbled over Rocky. He was busily engaged in gnawing the table leg. In amazement she heard the wood crunch as he literally bit a large chunk from it in one bite.

"Can you believe that?" she asked in amazement. Gesturing about her, she pointed to the remnants of several of her macrame hangers. "This guy is a real disaster," she said, laughing. "What other puppies do to shoes he does to the entire house."

"I believe it," Matt said, joining in her laughter and

glad to have found a comfortable topic of conversation. "These dogs really were developed to fight in the pit and they sometimes have a force of more than a thousand pounds of pressure in their jaws. Bones and wood are like paper in those teeth."

"You know," she said companionably, "they really are amazing animals, aren't they? Their history is so brutal and yet they seem to be so genuinely gentle. . . ."

"Yes, they are," he said, warming to the subject and once again relaxed. "In the beginning, from what I've read, there were just a few dogs like this. Someone way back when must have gotten bored with his medieval existence and discovered that watching animals fight was exciting in a sadistic sort of way. Really though, I guess people have always done it, the Romans, everyone. Before long they began to identify with the winners—some sort of alter-ego thing, I guess—and that led into gambling. In domesticating animals we usually try to breed gentleness into them, but these guys went in the exact opposite direction. They looked for the meanest and sturdiest animals they could find and then baited them to encourage them to fight one another. When they had one that would stay and fight almost to death at their bidding, under their command, they were in their glory."

Irene thought she sensed a note of disgust as Matt ended this long, rather matter-of-fact dialogue.

"It does seem like a giant step backward," she mused.

"Yes, it was," he said with emphasis. Matt seemed to have thoughtfully immersed himself in this discussion. For a moment Irene thought he had forgotten she was there. Then he looked over to her. "I've spent months learning about them. I guess they are an offshoot of the old bull- and bear-baiting days in England and these dogs are mixed and matched crosses of some of the original bulldogs—oh, but I'm probably boring you to death," he said, suddenly contrite.

"Not at all," Irene said sincerely. "This is fascinating. As a matter of fact I have a book here someplace. Wait just a minute and I'll find it." As she rose, her natural clean scent, touched with a hint of light, flowery cologne, wafted about her. In the shadows of the setting evening she felt truly at peace.

"Here it is," she said, returning. "Let's see, they list the English bulldog, that ugly brute we are all familiar with. From what it says they were first used primarily to bait bulls. She shuddered. "Makes you wonder, doesn't it?" she mused.

Matt returned her gaze and they moved a little closer together as they browsed through the pages of the book companionably. In the succeeding pages there was a variety of dogs, most of them similar in appearance. They sported low-slung square bodies with ordinary-looking heads that were differentiated only by the nose, which came in various degrees of bluntness and extension. There were numerous references to their agility, clownishness, loyalty, and courage.

Turning another page they came to the American Staffordshire terrier. The picture was the exact duplicate of Rocky except that the dog pictured was brown with a blaze of white splashed from the nose down to the front feet. "That's Rocky," Irene said. She noted, however, that while color wasn't specific, all white was not encouraged, which meant that Rocky wouldn't be terrifically good as a show dog.

"But he's not," Matt broke in, almost as if he read her thoughts, "an American Staffordshire terrier. Rocky is an American pit bull terrier—which some believe to be a cross between this dog and the bull terrier." He turned the page to show her the latter. He was obviously familiar with this book too. "You see," he went on, "dogfighting was legal here in the States until 1932. The American pit bull terrier was developed in this country and it's still used in the illegal pits today."

As they sat on the low porch divan in the dim light their bodies had slowly and companionably begun to meld together. A small shaft of imperceptible inner pleasure went through Irene as she became aware of the strength of Matt's thigh so close to her own. Their eyelashes were within inches of giving fanciful butterfly caresses to one another as they continued to pore over the book. Not altogether impervious to the promise of further sweet intimacies, Matt broke the magic of the moment as he looked away and continued in a somewhat husky voice.

"This is strictly an AKC standards book," he said, examining the cover. "They don't recognize the American pit bull terrier. I'll bring you a copy of the standards from UKC tomorrow if I can remember it. You did say you wanted that info anyway, didn't you?"

"Oh, yes," Irene said. "This really is very interesting. I've never had any reason to go into this before, and I guess, really . . . the whole idea of pitting two animals against each other is so disgusting to me—the dogs in a way were too. . . ."

Realizing she was suddenly treading in deep water as a speculative, somewhat accusatory look flashed across Matt's face, Irene sought to quickly extricate herself from this incriminating admission.

"But, Rocky," she went on, "is such a love. It seems a shame that such wonderful animals, obviously developed for all of the wrong reasons, should be forever maligned because of their background."

"I agree completely. That's exactly why I've gotten involved." He grinned and gave her arm a comradely squeeze. "Aside from the fact," he continued, "that they are such clowns and acrobats that it is almost like being at a circus when they play."

"You really have a point there," she said, joining him in laughter.

Almost as if choreographed for the moment Rocky and Buffy came bursting through the door again. They had been in an almost constant frolic in and around the house and porch throughout the conversation between Irene and Matt.

For once Buffy seemed to have the upper hand. He had apparently found a small, hard round steak bone and Rocky was chasing him madly. As they bobbed around, Buffy nonchalantly sniffed around and finally selected a spot to settle in not far from Irene's feet. Completely impervious to Rocky's presence, Buffy began to gnaw and nibble on the bone, which he held secure in his front paws.

To the amazement of Matt and Irene, Rocky dropped down in front of Buffy and stretched out parallel with his nose not more than six inches from the smaller dog. He began to beg with a deep guttural moan sliding to a high-pitched whine as he contorted his huge body impatiently. It was obvious that he could have broken the little dog in two with just one good snap of those powerful jaws, but to the continued amazement of Irene and Matt he chose to roll to his back, flailing his legs in anguish as he continued to emit painful moans and whines, demanding that he be given a turn with the bone too. Buffy was supreme in his enjoyment of the moment and gave no indication of any intent to share.

Laughing, Irene said, "Something tells me that Rocky would be a real cur."

"Don't kid yourself," Matt said a little too quickly. In a flash their companionable, relaxed mood dissipated. "It just takes one real encounter and all of their inbred tendencies quickly begin to surface."

Irene looked at him dubiously as a tinge of her old concern and suspicions whispered to her subconscious.

"You never know when it might come out," Matt added, "what with all the nuts out there who don't know what they are doing, breeding them with God knows what. Some of these dogs are getting a little wacky. Recently there have been cases of them not only injuring other animals but people as well."

Irene could feel herself growing pale.

"Not long ago," he said meaningfully, "they killed a little kid. The dogs belonged to his father."

"But that's crazy," cried Irene. "Rocky is just a big playful baby. Never, not even from the beginning when most dogs would have had a big territorial fight, has he ever threatened Buffy. He's just a big comedian and if he ever got near the pit he'd be creamed in one second."

"He would, would he?" Matt quizzed thoughtfully. He seemed to be a little annoyed.

Suddenly Matt grabbed a pillow and shot it into a corner of the screened porch with a familiar football pass motion.

"Get him!" he shouted.

In a flash a deep growl erupted from Rocky and he was on top of the pillow. In seconds he had ripped it to shreds and a blizzard of foam filled the corner. His teeth locked through a large piece of the filler and saliva poured down the sides of his mouth as he continued to growl menacingly while he pinned it to the ground and stood over it in a rigid, four-legged widespread stance, every muscle in his body tensed.

The whole thing had happened in less than thirty seconds. Buffy, suddenly aware of the change in atmosphere, left his bone and began to yap excitedly while running around Rocky, careful, however, to keep his distance, ready for yet another game.

70

"Stop that!" cried Irene. "What are. you doing?" she shouted accusingly at Matt.

Feeling threatened by the little dog's presence Rocky growled in his direction while still maintaining his death grip on the pillow. Buffy instinctively cowered, realizing that this was not a game, and ran beneath the divan seeking protection.

Quickly Matt stepped over to Rocky and expertly inserted his thumbs in back of the dog's jaws. "Break it up," he said softly. "Break it up."

Slowly Rocky relaxed and dropped the pillow, looking a little sheepish, almost as if he were coming out of a hypnotic trance.

"What do you think you are doing?" shouted Irene. She was shaking with anger.

Rocky came to her, head down and ears back, seeking her forgiveness as he nudged her hand. His eyes registered confusion.

"I'm trying to show you that no matter how laughably gentle, loyal, and playful these dogs are," Matt said meaningfully, "they can still be very dangerous."

His dark eyes were very serious and penetrating, willing her to understand, but she rejected his appeal.

"Some of them are literal time bombs. Sometimes play turns into an instinctive attack if they haven't had proper conditioning and they're not under the control of an enlightened owner."

"But you deliberately provoked him!"

"You know, for someone as intelligent as I think you are," he said as he paused to catch his breath, "you are also dangerously naive." He gestured expansively toward the kennel. "You've got a kennel full of dogs and people coming around here all of the time. You don't know what their real attitudes toward animals are."

Still commanding that her eyes meet his, he went on

71

pointedly. "You're lucky that what just happened hasn't happened before. Some of these guys around here will see that dog and they won't be able to resist seeing what he will do. Anyone could have said what I just did and the result might have been the same."

Looking over at Rocky, who was now panting quietly at Irene's feet, Matt continued. "If I hadn't known how to handle him someone could have gotten hurt. Rocky obviously has a very aggressive tendency when challenged. The jaws of these dogs are so powerful that when they are in battle the handlers have to use 'break sticks' to get them apart. You need to know what you are dealing with," he ended sternly.

Irene could feel anger overtaking her again. All of her previous suspicions about Matt had not only surfaced, but were further fueled and all the more infuriating because he was making her feel foolish.

"And just what makes you such an expert?" she spit out.

"I told you," he said calmly, ignoring the heat of her outburst completely, "I've spent a great deal of time learning about these dogs. I think it is highly irresponsible to become involved with an animal that has had such a volatile background and not know what you are dealing with. The whole game, you know, is genetics and breeding. Pit bulls are basically wonderful animals and I hate to see them manipulated to the point of destruction. Someone has to care enough to protect them."

He paused a few seconds and then continued, hesitantly, introspectively, totally disregarding Irene's presence. "I had another pit bull once, a very special one, before I got involved with Rocky. I lost him because he wasn't adequately protected. . . ."

His speech had become almost academic, but it was also

touched with a note of fervor. Again Irene looked at him in puzzlement.

Seeing her expression, Matt quickly changed his demeanor, giving the decided impression that he suddenly felt as though he had said something out of place. "Look," he said, breaking into a forced grin, "I'm sorry. We were having such a marvelous day. I didn't mean to upset you this way. I guess I'm as bad as some of those other guys." He scratched his head and looked at her somewhat impishly. "I really just acted on an impulse. I guess I'm as surprised as you are by Rocky's reaction, and then . . . well, it scared me too."

He seemed to will her to forgive him as he continued his obviously contrived, lighthearted explanation. "You are lucky, I guess, that Buffy seems to have become Rocky's instant 'familiar'—you know, like some racehorses who establish a bond between a goat or chicken. It happens in high-strung animals all the time."

Walking over to her, he looked at her intently and Irene could feel the room beginning to sway. He reached out to pat her shoulder and the warmth of his fingers radiated confusion throughout her body.

"I really do think," he said gently, "you should keep Rocky away from other animals until we've had more time to work with him—to see just how extensive and deep-rooted his aggression is. As far as he was concerned, he was playing today. Right now he's confused. So what do you say I take him out for a run and reassure him?"

Before Irene could answer him, Matt was on the run and both of the dogs were tearing ahead of him in wild abandon, headed for the woods. As they all disappeared into the trees her emotions were in familiar turmoil, further heightened by the sweetness and camaraderie they had shared just before the unfortunate display of Rocky's aggression. Irene felt a desperate longing to believe in Matt. There was something about him that was very appealing and sincere. She sensed genuine gentleness, but her subconscious taunted her as it whispered, "He knows too much."

CHAPTER FIVE

"You never told me what you called him."

Matt and Rocky were lying breathless on the grass, trying to recover from the wild tussle they had just participated in. Irene was watching them fondly. Matt had been coming out for more than a week and this was usually the way he and the dog ended up after an hour or so of obedience and show-ring training. She had to admit that Matt was very skillful and Rocky was responding beautifully.

"Oh, am I to assume," Matt said with exaggerated theatrics, "that you are actually admitting that this is my dog?"

"Not at all," she said, responding in kind. "What I meant to say was that you had never told me the name of the dog that you lost."

"You will play your games, won't you?" His eyes crinkled as he leisurely appraised her. "You are without a doubt the most independent, willful, tenacious woman I have ever encountered."

Irene laughed a great, joyous laugh of derision. She had,

at last, come to feel very comfortable with Matt during these past few days. She had watched him as he worked with the animals, not only Rocky but the animals in the kennel as well. He gave her a hand if things happened to be a little hectic when he was around.

Irene had always instinctively believed in that old saying about kids and animals being the best judge of character. Matt had exhibited a full array of emotions in her presence; firmness, tenderness, joy, annoyance, but never, ever cruelty—not even a hint of it. Now they had managed to establish a relaxing and refreshing rapport. She honestly looked forward to his visits and had even convinced herself that her physical response to him had mellowed out and was, in fact, a healthy manifestation. Their original abrasivness was now more a challenge of wits. Neither, however, ever alluded to that one fleeting, innocent caress when they had been so tenderly close that first evening on the porch.

"To answer your question," Matt continued very matter-of-factly, "Rocky's real name is an unbelievable conglomeration." He began a playful roughhouse mime with the dog, who was lying submissive and unguarded. "Rocky suits him well," he said as the dog responded playfully. "About the only sensible name in the lot was 'Carver.' "

"I see," said Irene. "You know, that reminds me that you never brought those UKC standards out. I really wanted to see them.".

"Still don't trust me, huh?" he said, laughing, but Irene thought she sensed a touch of annoyance too.

"You said it," she rebounded. "But seriously, I'm really interested now. I never paid much attention to that registry other than knowing that it existed."

"Matt? Are you here?"

A woman's strident voice was suddenly calling from the

front of the house. Before Matt could respond Lola came striding around the house. She was, as always, in tight jeans, heavily made-up, and her platinum hair bobbed freely in the current popular frowsy style. Her eyes were flashing fire as she looked from Matt to Irene.

"Have you forgotten we have an important meeting tonight?" she demanded. She was a picture of consternation as she stood, hands on hips, glaring at Matt.

He flashed her a look of annoyance. "You know I wouldn't do that," he said. "I was just finishing up here. I'll be with you in just a moment."

Matt gestured a "c'est la vie" shrug to Irene, which she suspected was a chauvinistic attempt to save face as he slowly arose, brushing grass from his pants. He wasn't the type of man who would respond well to such an address, as well Irene knew. He often walked out to the kennel and usually Lola came around to pick him up. He had made no explanation about her except to state simply that she was a friend. Usually, however, in spite of her appearance, Lola had been submissive and quiet, saying little more than hello and good-bye; quite the opposite of this demanding, possessive woman who was impatiently tapping her foot.

"It would help," Lola said meaningfully to Matt, "if you would try to keep your mind where it belongs." She glared at Irene.

Irene was completely bewildered. Sure, she suspected Lola was something more than just a "friend," but this was so out of character. After all, she certainly wasn't inviting Matt out here. He was here at his own insistence. She didn't appreciate this kind of insinuation and was about to tell them both so when Matt broke in.

"Go to the truck, Lola." His voice was very quiet and deliberate. "I know exactly what I am doing, and you do too."

The sound of his voice was chilling. It suddenly seemed very apparent to Irene that Matt was quite capable of being cruel. Lola had turned with a defiant toss of her head to return to the truck. He remained silent until she had disappeared around the house.

Matt turned back to Irene. She was clasping herself protectively, obviously appalled by this incident.

"I'm sorry," he said, his voice once again warm, carefully controlled with concern. "Sometimes Lola gets a little nervous and she tends to overreact." He willed her eyes to meet his. "Please forget that this ever happened."

Irene looked away, fearful that tears would betray her inner emotions. She realized that she was hurt. He had managed to pierce the shield she had constructed so carefully and he was wounding her deeply. He took a step toward her, but she willed herself to recover and her cold eyes stopped him. "Lola is waiting," she said meaningfully as she turned and walked away.

Moments later Irene heard the truck roaring down the drive. When she walked through the door of the chalet the phone was ringing. As she turned dazedly to respond to it she was in a tumult both physically and emotionally. She had begun to feel as though she were on an emotional roller coaster that was never going to stop. When she picked up the phone a male voice, confident and exuberant, addressed her.

"Irene? David Thornton here." There was a tiny, perceptible pause before he went on, but not long enough to allow her to respond. "How are you today?"

"Oh, fine . . . fine," she stammered as she rapidly adjusted back to her normal composure. She nevertheless required a big breath as she ran her hand through her long hair, brushing it back in abandon. Unconsciously her stance assumed a somewhat wary pose as she stood, one

78

leg extended, hand on hip, with the phone cradled between her neck and shoulder.

"That's great," he said, completing his canned salutation. "I was wondering—if you aren't busy this evening I'd like to run over and take a look at that new dog of yours, which I didn't have time to see the other day." His voice was smooth and suave, a study in courtesy.

Quickly, Irene tried to think of something to put him off. She wasn't up to another encounter today. The quixotic agitation of the past week was beginning to take its toll. Her nerves were beginning to take on a constant twangy-edged state that was more often present than not. David, however, was not only a prominent, respected man in the community, but also a big man in the dog circles. It would not pay professionally to be discourteous to him.

She was beginning to realize that her coveted peace was definitely beginning to slip away; even in moments of pure relaxation such as the one she had just been enjoying with Matt before the shattering appearance of Lola. The threat of an ever-present subconscious tension hovered, keeping her constantly on edge.

It was becoming increasingly necessary to consciously monitor her responses to others. Sporadically a sharp note had begun to creep into her voice, which was usually warm and melodious, only to be replaced by a note of high euphoria depending on the trauma of the moment and, more truthfully, the status of her rapport with Matt Davis; something that after this last episode she was beginning to resent very much.

In the seconds that these thoughts flashed through her mind Irene collected herself sufficiently to reply to David warmly.

"Why, certainly, David. I'd be delighted."

"Wonderful," he responded. "Shall we say about six? Will you be free then?"

"Six is fine," she confirmed in a lilting voice.

As she replaced the phone she gave a great sigh, searching for sustenance from her deep inner resources. This dipping into that personal reservoir that she had carefully filled through astute analysis of all the therapeutic doctrines designed to assist in coping with the tensions of a modern, independent woman, was getting to be a regular thing again. She had honestly felt that she had put most of that behind her once she had reconciled herself to the reality of her marital status and ultimately realized that her entire existence had, on the whole, improved. She was truly content and happier than she had ever been before, secure with her personal sense of self-respect.

The advent of Matt Davis, however, and her commitment to save Rocky had effectively dislodged her complacency. Rocky, by himself, might not have been so bad. Her smugness was, in reality, beginning to hint at a touch of boredom. It was good to have something that stirred your blood and fired your enthusiasm. A passionate commitment, within reason, to a worthy cause never hurt anyone.

Matt, however, was a totally different ballgame. Her reaction to him was childish. He had in no way indicated any kind of committed interest in her other than veiled suggestions through casual banter. She still knew nothing about him, other than that he insisted that Rocky was his and he worked for a construction company somewhere in Cramdon.

He never called. He just showed up. His priority and sole reason for coming around was Rocky. His obvious relationship with Lola and his arrogance in flaunting her so casually in front of Irene was decidedly insulting, but only in the context of her own personal standards, Irene had to admit. Such relationships were routinely accepted in most instances today and only a completely unsophisticated prude would issue censure.

No, this was entirely her own doing, the result of an overworked imagination, prone to fantasy and obviously not enough exposure to more appropriate, available men. Perhaps David was just what she needed right now. Irene had met him at several kennel club meetings. She had had dinner with him a few times and they had discussed getting together more often, but she had been so busy during those first hectic months that while she had made friends, she had honestly not had the time or energy to socialize to any great extent. David had just sort of faded away until his unexpected appearance the other morning. He had, however, always been warm and friendly, the personification of a southern country gentleman, and he obviously admired Irene very much. She, in turn, had found his company sophisticated and amusing.

As she headed for the bedroom to change, Irene glanced at the clock and realized that she had time for a relaxing soak. She chose one of her favorite bath oils and dropped her soggy kennel clothes in a mound as the room began to fill with steam from water pouring into the sunken hot tub she had installed rather than the standard bathtub. It was surrounded with attractive rustic decking, and an abundance of healthy plants were also nurtured there. Floor-to-ceiling windows, veiled by a loosely worked macrame hemp curtain, looked out onto the thick forest, giving the illusion of a natural spring in a forest glen, completely secluded and private. Discreetly tucked away next to it was a standard shower. Irene loved to dash from the tub into the shower for a bracing icy rinse provided by the subterranean spring water that she used throughout the house for all of her water needs.

She scrubbed leisurely and began to feel the tensions floating away as the whirling waters of the tub worked their magic. As the events of the day began to take on a proper perspective Irene found herself growing amused. *I must have been quite a picture,* she thought. The discomfiture of Matt trying to handle two ruffled females at the same time suddenly became absolutely hilarious to her. She began to laugh, wildly and heartily at first, and then, uncontrollably, until the laughter gave way at last to tears tinged with a bittersweet merriment.

Slowly she got out of the tub, still chuckling to herself, and began drying herself with a thick, luxuriant towel. Her movements resembled those of a slow, sensuous massage as her skin began to tingle. She felt wonderfully refreshed as she opened the closet and selected a bright, gay caftan and golden thong sandals. Deftly she twisted her hair into a sophisticated knot and applied discreet makeup that subtly highlighted her face and gave her a polished "haute couture" look that suited her well.

As she finished with a spray of her favorite light cologne she heard the doorbell ring accompanied by the barking alarms of Rocky and Buffy. Laughing, she weaved through the noisy dogs as she attempted to shush them. When she opened the door she was a picture of radiance in the tradition of Loretta Young from a bygone movie era.

"You look wonderful!" said David, obviously impressed. He openly admired her as he stepped through the door.

"Why, thank you," Irene said, appreciative of his praise. "I love working in the kennel all day, but I always enjoy the opportunity to relax in the evening."

"Well, I must say you certainly look lovely. If a man knew he could come home to someone looking like you every night, being a bachelor might not seem so attractive." He made the statement in obvious jest, but a hint of seriousness also hovered in the air.

"You joke," she said in light response, "but I love it. Could I fix you a drink?"

82

David's eyes widened in pleasure. He had not expected this. "Indeed you may," he said enthusiastically. "In fact, I had rather hoped that we might have that dinner date we have discussed so often, but I didn't wish to be too presumptuous." He ended with a twinkle in his eye.

"Of course we can," Irene responded warmly as she began to rattle bottles in the bar. "I'm afraid today has been a little hectic, but I'll take a rain check for Saturday if you're game."

She spoke brightly and looked at him directly, but nevertheless managed to exude an aura of refined demureness that gave her a hint of mystery and ultrasophistication. "Now tell me what you drink."

"Bourbon and water is fine and Saturday would be wonderful," he replied, a look of satisfaction clearly evident on his face. "But let's get on with the subject of my visit this evening. Is this your new dog?" He gestured toward Rocky, who was panting heavily and watching him quizzically from his usual lopsided stance. His eyes seemed to wince in acknowledgment when he heard his name.

Bottle and glasses chinked softly as Irene went about preparing their drinks. She had decided that she would enjoy bourbon and water too.

"Yes," she said in answer to his question about Rocky. She handed his drink to him. "Oh, forgive me," she said as she gestured around the room. David had remained standing and Irene realized that she had not invited him to sit down. "Please make yourself comfortable."

Quickly David settled himself in the large chair next to Rocky. "Thank you," he said as he took the drink. He took a sip and savored it as he carefully appraised the dog. "He looks like a very good dog," he said after a moment. Rocky did not respond to him in any way. He remained in his "sit" position and watched the man carefully. "But unfortunately someone has done a rather poor job with those ears."

Irene was instantly alert. "You know, of course, that I found him," she stated matter-of-factly. She now assumed that everyone was aware of her business. This small-town characteristic had become quite apparent during the past week. "Matt Davis, the fellow you met the other day, tried to claim him, but as he mentioned, we have come to an agreement. He wants to show him in the UKC show this summer. Rocky's ears still had the stitches in them when I found him, but now they seem to have healed very well."

"Yes, well, it is a matter of some debate, but the true fanciers of these dogs usually opt to leave the ears in their natural state," he said. His reasonable lawyer debate voice was suddenly evident.

"I can certainly understand that," Irene said meaningfully. "Personally I think cropping any dog's ears is an unnecessary, painful procedure, but I suspect Rocky's ears were cropped for other revolting reasons." There was a little shake in her voice as her inner feelings momentarily surfaced.

David took a long sip of his drink as he silently gazed at her in reflective consideration.

"My dear, if you are saying what I think you are saying, you are most grievously and erroneously misinformed about the true destiny of these wonderful animals and the people who believe in them and are in fact responsible for their continued existence."

Irene was completely taken aback. This was the last thing she had expected to hear from David Thornton tonight.

"When I say fancier," he went on with just a note of condescension in his voice, "I am talking about the people who breed them, train them, and manage them for one of the most noble exercises in courage man or beast might ever participate in."

She looked at him silently, shocked, not believing what she was hearing.

"Don't look so shocked, my dear," David said suddenly conscious of her reaction. "You are obviously suffering from the delusions that animal welfare groups have insisted on fostering in their efforts to sensationalize a legitimate sport that is no worse than boxing, strictly for the purpose of filling their own coffers. Their survival depends upon donations and people only give when they think the organization is trying to stop something that is heinous and terrible."

His voice was reasonable. In that moment Irene found it hard to believe that a considerate, genteel man such as David could possibly be supporting something that was, in fact, grotesque.

"Truthfully," he asked earnestly, "tell me just how much you know about this firsthand."

She looked at him blankly. Actually Irene had to admit that her entire knowledge was based on hearsay, flyers, and articles she had read in newspapers and magazines. There was no way, though, that this business could be anything but grisly—on the same level as white slavery or any other activity that utilized unwilling victims.

"The ears, for example," David said, taking advantage of her silence to prove his point. "Most people think dog sports crop the ears to prevent serious injury in the pit, when the exact opposite is usually true. The old-timers believe that the ear intact is strategically more advantageous simply because a nip in the tip of the ear is not at all damaging."

Irene visibly shuddered. This was without a doubt the most unexpected and shocking conversation she had ever participated in, yet somehow David's arguments seemed reasonable and objective to some degree. Never, though, could she agree that the animals were not in pain and she could not sanction that possibility.

As the comments about the cropping of the ears began to sink in, however, Irene suddenly felt an almost euphoric sense of relief as almost the entire basis of her suspicions of Matt dissipated.

"Are you saying, then, that dogs' ears are not usually cropped for this activity?"

"Oh, sure they are," David said, relieved to see that she was willing to participate in the conversation, "but usually only newcomers who aren't really knowledgeable do it, although I have to admit some of the old-timers swear by it too. It really is a matter for debate, but the real pros today usually don't do it."

Irene's euphoria instantly crashed about her. These last comments provided damning support for all of her earlier suspicions of Matt. Shakily, she began to realize the full implications of the conversation. "David," she said, genuinely concerned, "are you actually telling me you are involved in something that is illegal?"

"You know, one of the greatest shames I can think of in a supposedly free country is the interference of big government in local affairs, especially when that self-righteous bureaucracy takes no consideration of the real facts." David spoke earnestly and fervently. "This entire country," he went on, "worships violence—in the movies, on the football fields, at hockey games, and, most graphically of all, in the boxing ring. All of those things are revered and declared sports, yet the motivation behind watching them is exactly the same for those who truly enjoy our noble sport."

"But the participants in those activities," Irene responded, "choose to do so and they are protected. They are not grievously injured. . . ." She finished lamely as she realized a cursory glance at any sports page made a mockery of her words.

"That's precisely the point," David said in recognition of her unspoken realization. "These animals have been bred for combat and they love it. It is their destiny," he finished passionately.

There were all sorts of comments she could make, but David's passion was obviously akin to that of a Spanish bullfight afficionado and Irene knew her arguments would be useless.

"To answer your question," David continued quietly, "as a lawyer I am deeply offended by the presumptuous labeling that a group of fanatics has managed to accomplish through these unjust laws. But our world here, and most especially around Cedarville, is our own private community. The officials here have other more important concerns. They rarely bother those of us who have battled to maintain the sport at its highest plane."

"I really don't know why you are telling me all of this, David." Irene was growing decidedly more uncomfortable with each passing minute. This was obviously not a relationship that she could encourage either. Yet there was something winning about David, and she felt a genuine sense of regret.

"I had no intention of discussing this with you," he said candidly. "I guess perhaps I'm getting a little reckless, but I'm also getting tired of having something that is essentially harmless, when conducted properly, maligned simply because, thanks to all of the sensational publicity the animal welfare groups have generated, it has attracted a lot of unsavory characters. I am the first to admit the animals they are involved with are often misused and abused."

Irene had to admit that she was somewhat confused. David seemed to be representing an entirely different facet of this issue and he did so in a reasonable and eloquent way.

"I'm afraid, David, I really do find this most difficult to understand. I have seen pictures of animals mortally and horrendously injured from battles that lasted for hours. Are you actually saying that you participate, but that your animals are not injured?"

"In a way, yes," he answered. "Before we go out to dinner Saturday night I'd like to have you come up to Greentree, my estate, and see my wonderful, brave dogs, all of which have seen combat and all of which are healthy. They have sustained injuries in their battles, but nothing they couldn't handle, the same as a football player or boxer. Our 'matches' are designed to exhibit the gameness of the dogs, all of which have been carefully bred and selected for temperament. We don't allow them to sustain crippling injuries—the dogs are too valuable to us. A lot of them are our personal pets, the same as your Rocky here."

Irene gasped inwardly as she recalled their earlier agreement to have dinner. She tried to think of some way to extricate herself gracefully without insulting David. He had obviously taken her into his confidence and perhaps a little too quickly felt he had persuaded her to consider his rational explanations about dogfighting.

Sensing her confusion, David sought to further reassure her. "Actually, the reason I'm coming out of the woodwork, so to speak," he offered, "is because I and several others in my group are considering the sponsorship of a lobby that would present the true picture and allow this to become a legitimate, regulated sport just like all of the others we've discussed. We'd like to see the riffraff and other bad elements destroyed, too. So long as this activity is underground and illegal, those elements are going to be attracted to it and they are corrupting and desecrating a noble contest."

Irene's head was beginning to spin. In her quest to combat one conflict she had somehow unwittingly exposed herself to yet another. She was impressed with David's idealistic, ethical stand, but that did not in any way negate the horrendous realities of this depraved activity; she was sure of that.

"David, I don't think I am capable of discussing this with any real objectivity. . . . You will have to forgive me, but just the thought of this is completely barbaric to me."

"Oh, my dear, do forgive me." He was effusively contrite and concerned. "I have been unforgivably presumptuous. Of course you can't possibly relate to what I am saying until you have actually witnessed firsthand what I am very inadequately trying to convey. I insist that you come up Saturday, for no other reason than to set your mind at ease."

Irene smiled at him weakly and realized it would do no good to try and refuse now. She would call him later and bow out.

"When you have seen the grace and beauty and the genuine strength of these dogs, I'm telling you even the bull entering the bullring with those first arrogant, commanding strides does not compare. It is truly an honor to own such an animal and feel that it is a part of you. Watching them makes me feel wonderful."

David's voice had taken on a hint of fanaticism that left Irene feeling uneasy. They had both finished their drinks and Irene did not offer him another. Their discussion had had very little to do with Rocky, who had, in fact, managed to stay completely in the background throughout their conversation. Irene was hoping David would take the hint and leave soon. She was beginning to feel completely exhausted.

Perceptive to her feelings, David gave her a big smile and extended his hand as he arose. "Thanks, my dear, for the drink and the company," he said. "Again I apologize, if I have upset you in any way. . . ."

"Not at all," she lied prettily. "In its own way our conversation was rather fascinating. You certainly present this in an entirely different light."

"Then, shall I pick you up, say, around three on Saturday? Would that be convenient?"

"I . . . I guess so," she said. Irene could have kicked herself. Hadn't her mother always told her honesty was the best policy? If this had been Matt Davis who was talking to her this way she would have had him thrown in jail by now. What was so different about David? Somehow she just couldn't bring herself to refuse him.

"See you then," he said debonairly. "If you so desire we can have dinner at Greentree or one of the better spots in town—whatever you wish."

Before Irene could speak again he was out the door with a final sophisticated "ciao." She stared after him blankly.

"Something tells me you are blowing this," she said out loud. Hearing her voice alone, the dogs came to join her. Slowly and playfully she tousled their ears, once again cognizant of the vast differences in the soft silkiness of Buffy's and the unnatural rigidity of Rocky's. Who would have believed that her original observation would plunge her into such a mess?

CHAPTER SIX

She had had another fitful night, and everything that could possibly go wrong in the kennel the next day, did. When Irene finally stepped out the kennel door, she was nearly overturned by Rocky, who was in hot pursuit of a cat.

"Rocky!" she shouted. Where on earth was Matt? The only way the dog could be loose like this was if Matt had come while she was busy inside and let him out. She was furious that he would allow the dog to do such a thing.

"Rocky!" she shouted again as the cat mercifully made it up a tree. It was completely frantic and by the state of its coat had barely escaped the dog's powerful jaws.

"Oh, there you are," she said accusingly as she turned and almost ran into Matt. "Why are you allowing Rocky to chase that cat?" she demanded.

"He wasn't doing anything that any other dog wouldn't do," he said, unperturbed. "You can't always hold them in or you'll end up breaking their spirit completely."

"Poppycock," she spit out.

Apparently he was just coming back and taking up

where he had left off, as though absolutely nothing had happened the day before.

"I've seen you handling animals and there is nothing you are incapable of training them to do," she continued hotly. "After that episode with Rocky on the porch the other day I thought we had agreed that it was in everyone's best interests to condition and control his latent aggressive characteristics! Don't you care about what might have happened to the cat?"

"Of course I care," he said in annoyance. "I was after him. He just slipped me for a moment."

Somehow Irene found this extremely hard to believe. Matt's control over Rocky was almost like iron. In fact, she found it hard to believe that Rocky had committed this act without some active encouragement.

"This is just inexcusable!" she sputtered. "If you can't control him better than this I think we will have to definitely rethink this arrangement."

"Now, I don't want to get into that again," he said impatiently. With a shrug, he dismissed it completely as he reached into his shirt pocket and withdrew some folded papers. "These are the standards you were asking about yesterday. You know, from the UKC," he said in response to her rather quizzical look.

She was still very angry and Matt had switched tracks so quickly that she had, for a moment, found it hard to follow him.

"Oh . . . yes," she said as she shook her head impatiently in an effort to clear it. "Put them there on the desk in the kennel lobby. I don't have time to look at them right now. I still have Galahad, that big old English sheepdog, to bathe." Returning to the original issue she spoke firmly. "I want you to promise me that something like this won't happen again."

"I told you it was an accident." His eyes were stormy and angry, but he spoke calmly.

Irene turned wordlessly and went back into the kennel to finish her work. The door slammed behind her with a loud rap as she reached resignedly for a strong slip leash. Slowly, almost dragging her feet, she walked to the end of the kennel, where a large, frisky old English sheepdog greeted her joyously. She slipped the leash easily over his large head, which was so profusely covered with long hair that his eyes, ordinarily invisible, were momentarily uncovered as the rope brushed the hair aside. They peeped at her, impish and filled with eagerness, as his peculiar "pot-casse" bark rang out loudly. The dog danced in anticipation as she fumbled impatiently with the kennel door, creating a comedic illusion of a shaggy animated rug. His joy was infectious, and Irene soon found herself responding lightheartedly to him as she matched his characteristic smooth-paced walk toward the bathing area next to the lobby.

As they neared the tub Irene realized that the dog was really much too large for her to lift alone into the standard bathtub, which had been installed so that the top edge was counter level. Washing this dog was not, in any event, going to be an easy matter. His entire body was profusely covered with long hair, four to six inches long. Beneath that he still retained his undercoat, which was a waterproof pile. It would take at least an hour to comb him out, that is if she ever got him into the tub in the first place.

Ordinarily this was a service that would have cost the owner a minimum of twenty dollars if it had been done in a regular grooming shop, but Irene didn't have very many tenants such as Galahad and the bath at the end of every dog's stay was one of the nice touches that made her boarding business so successful.

As she perused Galahad's size once more, Irene remembered the ramp that the architect had suggested be installed next to the tub, with a counter top over it when not in use, for just such instances as this. She had thought that it was just another additional expense, which she didn't think was really neccessary. There was nearly always someone around to help—she usually planned it that way —but today Jeff was gone for the day and Matt was busy outside with Rocky. More importantly she was still smarting after the incident of a few moments ago and had no desire to call him for assistance. She bridled at the very thought of it, especially when she coupled this last incident with his exit from the day before.

"Galahad, you and I are going to do this together." She laughed as his eyeless Muppet head tilted quizzically toward her. She knew that if he had a tail it would be frantically wagging, but his gyrating body was indicative enough of in innate friskiness and anticipation.

Hearing his name, the dog, still clinging to remnants of his puppyhood, leaped forward, tilting his great body into a steep incline as his front legs dropped into a spraddled crouch position while the hind ones remained upright ready to spring him into action. His unique bark rang out again as he suddenly began to tear madly about the room, ripping the leash from Irene's hand in the process. Chairs and wastebaskets went flying as he slid and skittered about on the slick floor, his hair flying back in great bouncing, billowing waves. His face with the hair blown back was absolutely joyous as his pink tongue hung languidly from the side of his mouth and he beckoned Irene to join him in his fun.

"You come back here!" she said, laughing in spite of her frustration.

In a way this was going to be the end of a perfect day. Murphy's Law had reigned supreme all day and now she was going to spend the next two hours trying to catch and give a bath to a long-haired, playful brute who should have been a pony instead of a dog.

Galahad had been in the kennel for a week, and while he had been exercised every day he was used to the run of a huge yard. He looked now for a way to escape as he slowed down and began to examine the entry door.

Seeing that one good push would put the dog through the screen door, Irene realized the situation had become very serious. Losing an animal from the kennel was one of the most disastrous things that could possibly happen other than having an animal die.

She tried once more to reason with the dog. "Come here," she called softly as she began to advance slowly. She crouched so her eyes were level with the dog's, and although his were not visible she knew that he had her number and he was having none of this. He was too close to freedom.

Realizing that she had to do something quickly, Irene impulsively hurtled herself toward the dog and grabbed him in a flying tackle. They became a rolling tangle of hair, legs, and arms as they fell through the door and continued their wild scramble onto the lawn. Thinking he was in a game of games Galahad began to nip and growl playfully as his teeth snagged the edge of the sleeve on her blouse. He began to shake it in abandon. Afraid that he would get away, Irene ignored her ripping blouse and desperately clutched the dog around his great chest, locking her hands together. Her face was completely buried in his long hair as she tried frantically to find some purchase so she could regain control of the dog.

"Need any help?"

The laughter in his voice was not funny. Why did she forever seem to be in a compromising position when he was around? Anxiety and frustration gave way to instant fury as Irene felt Matt's strong arms go over hers and take command of the animal.

Irene and the old English sheepdog bursting through the door in such wild array had startled Matt, and he had come running after, quickly staking Rocky's leash into the ground. Now as he helped to untangle Irene from the dog he was overcome with the hilarity of the situation as the animal continued its frenzied attempt to gain freedom. The wide expanse of yard was too much to resist, but Galahad was no match for Matt's strength and Matt quickly had him under control.

Hot and sweaty, completely disheveled, Irene brushed her hair back and made an effort to smooth her clothes.

"I was just getting ready to give him a bath," she said matter-of-factly, forcing herself to keep a straight face. She refused to join Matt in his hilarious laughter.

"Looks like more of a wrestling match to me," he laughed, unable to control his amusement even though he knew by the way Irene looked his laughter was the same as lighting a match to her fuse.

Irene looked at him and realized he truly meant no harm. She was just infuriated that he had seen her in such a farcical, incompetent position.

"Are you okay?" he asked as he saw her visibly lighten up.

"Yes," she said sheepishly. "I guess we were quite a sight. Thanks. I would have lost him without your help."

"Let me help you get him inside." His words were tinged with laughter as his eyes continued to radiate his amusement.

They were just about to get the sheepdog through the door when suddenly from the corner of her eye Irene saw Rocky tearing toward them. He had managed to get his stake loose and was running madly to join in the fun.

"Oh, no!" she screamed.

Matt quickly pushed the large dog through the door as Irene shouted, "Don't let him get near Galahad!"

Turning, Matt quickly shouted a command to Rocky. "Stay!" Rocky instantly responded and looked almost as if he had run into a glass wall as he came to a screeching halt and then stood quietly, his heavy panting the only indication of his excitement. Striding quickly to him, Matt deftly secured the dog again and then turned to continue his assistance to Irene in her struggle with Galahad.

Matt saw the problem with the size of the dog and the position of the tub. "Why didn't you call me in the first place?" he said in exasperation.

"I didn't have a chance to," Irene said, not wanting him to know that she was foolishly trying to think of a way to get the dog into the tub by herself.

"Well, let's take care of that now," he said, as he turned on the spigots. Water gushed into the tub and Matt continued to gaze at her in amusement while firmly holding the leash of the agitated dog. When the water reached the halfway mark on the tub he tested it for warmness and said, "That looks pretty good. Stand back a second and I'll just heave-ho old Galahad here into the drink for you."

He turned to reach under the dog with both arms horizontally beneath the animal, allowing the body of the dog to rest on his strong arms while the legs of the animal hung freely over the outside of his arms. It was a classic animal-handling technique, but Galahad had decided this was definitely his day to be difficult. Before Matt could manuever him into the tub the dog began to struggle, and Irene quickly joined in to help. Together they finally landed the dog in the tub with a great splash as they fell against each other. Matt caught Irene closely in his arms and for a sweet second his lips hovered close to hers before the impatient Galahad required their full attention again.

"Think you can handle him now?" he asked huskily.

His fingers tenderly touched the ripped shreds of her sleeve but he said no more as he turned to leave.

"Yes, I think so," she said, her hands entwined firmly in the hair of the dog.

Once again she was aware of the warm gush that his presence always sent through her. She knew she was flushing again and hoped Matt would attribute it to the heavy exertion of handling the big animal.

"Okay, I'll see you later, then, but call me if you need any more help." Although his voice was authoritative he winked as he left.

Irene smiled and nodded her assent. "No problem," she said. "I don't usually have any trouble getting them out."

Within moments she was working the shampoo into the big dog, who was now docile and thoroughly enjoying himself. He soon looked like he was covered with fluffy seven-minute frosting. Rubbing and kneading the suds in expertly, Irene began to feel at one with the animal as they both enjoyed the relaxing scrubbing movements. When she grabbed the big wide spray head to start rinsing the long hair, Galahad instinctively gave a great shuddering shake, showering her completely with shampoo and water.

"You nerd," she said, as her laughter rang out joyously.

Matt had been about to reenter the kennel when he saw her working through the window. He stopped and stood quietly watching as she worked devotedly over the animal, and decided she could finish up with no further need of assistance. Slowly he turned and ran with Rocky toward the chalet. Irene had not seen him.

After a while Irene came into the rustic A-line shadows of the cozy great room of the chalet. "I don't know for sure who gave who a bath. That Galahad has got to be the biggest old English sheepdog with the longest hair of any I've ever seen . . ."

She thought she was talking to herself, but to her surprise Matt was in front of the fireplace. The day had suddenly, unaccountably, turned nippy again. He looked up at her from his crouch in front of it. The flames were catching and they illuminated the muscular hardness of his thighs and torso. That one small, stubborn tendril of hair had loosened again from his widow's peak as he gazed at her in appreciation.

She had changed into a fleecy robe that zipped up demurely and revealed the fineness of her body. Its creamy ecru color served to accent her tartan hair, which she had been drying with a towel as she talked. It tumbled about her head in total disarray as the nipples of her breasts matched the rhythm of her arms. She looked like a Renaissance porcelain statue suddenly come to life, full of fire. Unconsciously Matt's tongue slowly moistened his lips as he arose to greet her.

"Looks like it's going pretty good," he said, motioning to the fire. Noting the action of her breasts, his eyes deliberately, self-consciously avoided hers. "I thought you might enjoy a fire tonight after such a long day. It just took a minute. I thought I'd do it before I left and . . . I just wanted you to know I'm sorry about that incident with Rocky and the cat."

His sincerity was unquestionable. Irene realized that she may well have made him the brunt of her irritability from the day before, which had been compounded by an incredibly bad day today.

The aroma of soup from the slow cooker she had started early in the morning was mixing with the pungent aroma of the burning logs. Suddenly she realized she didn't want to spend the evening alone. She loved her chalet, but sometimes, because it was just the way she wanted it, it was almost unbearable not having someone with whom to share it. She looked at Matt, now flopped on the floor tussling with Rocky and Buffy as he reached for his hat near the fireplace.

"No need to go unless you want to," she said, indicating the soup in the small kitchen. "I've got enough soup there for an army. You are welcome to stay and have some with me." She ended a little awkwardly. Realizing what she was doing, she groped for a little more justification. "You earned it today—if it hadn't been for you I would have lost Galahad for sure, and I just," she went on a little lamely, "want you to know I really appreciate your help and . . . I'm sorry about my outburst over Rocky too."

"Glad to do it and just forget about it," he said exuberantly, as he arose and bounded toward her all in one motion. "That soup do-o-o smell good," he said in mock comic pantomime, "and you sure don't have to ask me twice!"

Irene was a little overwhelmed by this sudden exuberance, but in spite of herself a lilting giggle escaped from her as she went to get bowls from the cupboard. They enjoyed the savory vegetable soup with crisp crackers in companionable silence except for mirthful comments about Galahad's exploits. Both seemed happy to have restored the rapport established just a few days before.

"That was really fantastic," said Matt, as he finished his last spoonful. He sighed and sat back in his chair, patting his stomach in satisfaction. "You really are quite a little homebody, after all, aren't you?" he continued, looking at her appreciatively.

"Now just a minute," said Irene, suddenly irritated— why, she didn't really know, except she had worked hard to prove herself as something more than a domestic.

"Whoa!" said Matt in mock retreat, his hands coming up in front of him, palms out. "Don't go getting your hackles up. I meant that as a compliment!"

"Yes, of course you did," said Irene, rubbing her forehead. "It has been a long day and I guess maybe I'm a little strung out." She was a little ashamed now over her quick outburst and wanted to make it up. She was truly weary of confrontations. "What do you say we take our coffee in by the fire and just relax for a moment or two." Her voice was warm and companionable. Her eyes danced and played over Matt's face as a warm grin of acceptance crinkled his handsome tanned features.

"Why not, Fireball?" he said, grinning at her. "I don't think I've ever known anyone who could come so close to being a split personality and not be crazy, but then again . . ." he paused, teasing her.

"Oh, you . . ." she said in playful consternation. "Just move your bustle and quit picking on me. That's no way to treat someone who has just fed you and . . ." she continued coyly, "brought you in from the cold!"

"Picking on you!" he countered, matching her outraged banter as she swept past him toward the living room sofa in front of the fireplace. The toss of her hair, matching the sway of her hips, lured him enticingly as he settled next to her. As he took the hot mug from her, their fingers brushed.

"In from the cold," he continued in a somewhat lowered, husky banter, as he took a sip of the hot liquid and openly leered at her while grinning at the same time.

"Oh, God, it has been a long day," she said, sighing and falling back into the sofa, completely ignoring the implications of his sensuous teasing. She took a big sip from her cup and then arched her shoulders, reaching to massage her tired muscles. "And boy, am I tired."

She was completely relaxed and at ease now, appreciative of Matt's companionship. He no longer seemed to be some terrible threat. As the fire played over their faces Irene felt secure and safe with him, something she hadn't felt for a long time with anyone.

"Here," Matt said as he set his cup down, noting her feeble, ineffectual attempt at self-massage, "let me do that, you're not even close to the muscles that are really sore." His strong hands had reached over and began firmly but gently to knead her shoulders. It seemed so natural that Irene never even thought to demure and it did feel good.

"Ummm . . ." she moaned. She felt as though her body were beginning to float as the warmth of his hands began to penetrate, moving lightly and swiftly over her shoulders and up her neck. Her body swayed with them, yearning for more. Unconsciously she turned to him and his hands slid down her shoulders, coming around to cup her breast as his lips came down on hers, parting them deeply with his warm flickering tongue. Everything released within her as she pulled him down to her and parried with the force of his sweet, ravaging mouth.

Hesitating for just a second, Matt paused to check her reaction as he gazed at her intently and than began to caress her eyes softly. "You're lovely," he uttered, as his lips traveled gently over all of her features. Sensing her surrender, his hands began to move over the warm thickness of her robe. Slowly, while he held her and continued to kiss her deeply, one hand began to pull the zipper down gently until the warm softness of her breast grew taut and hard from the electricity of his big, gentle hand.

"Oh, baby, baby," he sighed, as his lips moved leisurely down her neck and hers brushed past the fringe of his eyelashes, reaching up to caress his ear while her white, dainty teeth began to tug playfully at its fleshy lobe. Her fingers reached up to ruffle his hair as he brushed her great mane back to once again seek out her lips. She was in ecstasy. Her hungry body felt the promise of his as his full weight came down on her and he gently began to remove her robe, hesitating only to devour her breast between his sweet, urgent lips. Slowly his hands played over her lean, supple body, moving ever lower, taunting and teasing as his fingers gently outlined her navel, causing every nerve in her body to tingle in urgency. His touch grew firmer as he outlined her thighs in a warm sensuous massage.

"Oh, Matt . . . oh, God, please it's been so long," she moaned. She began to tug at his shirt as her body undulated in anticipation and they began to move in unison toward the floor, which was bathed in firelight.

A yelp from an unsuspecting Rocky, who had settled at their feet, brought Irene suddenly to her senses and she was instantly mortified. Hastily pulling her robe back around her, she zipped it in a defiant motion and looked away from Matt's startled eyes.

"I'm sorry," she said bluntly. "I don't know what got into me. . . . This really isn't my style . . ." She looked around nervously to find words that would exonerate her, but none would come. "Please," she said finally, remembering that this was a man whom she really couldn't trust, no matter how he had acted in the past week or so. She still didn't know him or what he was up to. "Please, just go. This was a terrible mistake. . . ."

Seeing her anguish and self-chastisement, accompanied by a now obvious revulsion of him, Matt made no attempt to reason with her. Picking up his hat, he went silently toward the door, turning only to glance sadly at her rigid body, which was turned completely away from him. He pushed the door open and went out into the night air, while inside Irene began to hurt as she had never hurt before. Something told her this pain would never, ever, end. . . .

CHAPTER SEVEN

The crash of thunder and the flash of fierce lightning piercing through the tall windows of the bedroom awoke Irene from a fitful sleep. Buffy and Rocky were huddled next to her, safely ensconced with her in the bed. The forest around her seemed to be swirling through a giant egg beater as it whirled about her in a gigantic circular motion. Trees and bushes alike were bent and straining while great drops of rain bombarded thunderously against the windows. She felt singularly isolated, surrounded by an eerie calm, as though she were in the eye of a great storm unable to do anything except move along with its great wall of destruction.

Safe and snug, secure in her well-planned oasis, ordinarily she would have relished waking to such a day. It would have been a day to make soup, read by the fire, and in general bask in the comfort with which she had surrounded herself. Chalets were meant for days such as this, but as she began to move about she suddenly felt a great sense of suffocation.

The thought of returning to the living room, which she

had painfully left only a few hours before, filled her with such a great sense of chagrin that she was sure she could not emotionally survive it. The storm with all of its fury seemed far more comforting.

Hurriedly she went rummaging through her closet and soon found her old yellow rain slicker. She quickly grabbed warm woolen clothing and began to dress hastily. It was barely dawn, but she felt as though she had an appointment, as though the storm had arrived especially for her. Through its fury she could be cleansed, and perhaps it might assuage her emotions.

The dogs were bewildered. Rocky began to moan and whine as he slowly comprehended her intentions.

"Don't worry, you big brute," she said, "I'm not going to take you with me. Although I should—you're the one who got me into this mess!"

Quickly she stepped out the door and immediately felt a communion with the raging forces that surrounded her. Slowly she fought her way into the forest and immediately sensed a special abatement, as the intensity of the wind and water softly diminished through the natural filtering provided by the tall, dense trees.

It was lovely. The silence was poetic. The air was heavy and saturated with natural, moist woods aroma. She could taste the fresh clean wind. Walking leisurely she gazed upward, far more comfortable in this sanctuary than the one she had just left.

Slowly she relived the events of the evening before and openly petitioned for strength. How could she ever face him again? He had obviously been aware of her attraction to him right from the beginning and had simply awaited the opportunity that he knew would sooner or later present itself. There was no doubt in her mind as to what might have happened, had Rocky not been there. In her agony now, however, she really wasn't sure whether she

106

was sorry because of what happened or what didn't happen; but there was one thing she did know.

There was no use in trying to deny it any longer. She was in love with Matt Davis and she was just about to go through the meat grinder of fated, rejected love again. She had no alternative but to begin immediately to formulate a battle plan to ensure self-preservation.

It was crushing to realize just how poor her judgment was when it came to men, but that did not mean she had to be its victim again. She sat down on a huge tree stump and allowed herself to be immersed in the quiet world around her as the rain continued to fall softly. She stayed for more than an hour. When she finally emerged she felt greatly comforted and encouraged. She would survive. It was a simple matter of facing reality and then, not so simply, learning to live with it.

"Admit it," she told herself, "you have behaved worse than the frustrated town spinster in a small hick town who falls in love with the lion tamer in a traveling circus. You have allowed yourself to be attracted to a slick, stereotypical sexual image, the kind you see on TV every day, and then compounded it by covertly allowing yourself to be placed in a position of constant exposure." She allowed herself no mercy. "If you had really wanted to get rid of him, you could have," she chastised herself firmly. "You, alone, are to blame for this. He made you no promises, he offered you nothing, his relationship with Lola is obvious, and you are a victim of your own inability to control your own destiny. He is obviously some roguish vagabond who has nothing more to offer than his charm and magnetic attractivness. Women such as you are probably nothing more than breakfast appetizers in the course of his everyday existence."

Purposely Irene thought over their many varied conversations. They had run the gamut of anger and hysteria and teasing, comfortable banter, to thoughtful, provoking, academic discussions. They had been warm and electric. She had instinctively felt something special, only to have it instantly countered by his inconsistent and often inappropriate actions. It had been a sham from the beginning and she had made no effort to protect herself—that was painfully clear. It was also clear that she loved him.

She loved him passionately. Suddenly, with a piercing pang of comprehension, the face in her habitual dream became evident and she knew now why it had become such a comforting phenomena, contrary to the aggravation it once was.

"This has only been a few weeks out of your life," she continued firmly, "not two years. You can and you will handle this and you will survive."

When she finally reentered the chalet her confidence had returned and she once again felt proud of her accomplishments. Slowly she walked around the couch and tenderly touched the pillows, as his laughing eyes and tousled hair flashed before her. She remembered the tender kisses and her fiery, urgent surrender. She openly savored the best of the memory from the evening before. It was hers and she was entitled to it. It was all that she would ever have from this relationship.

Painfully, but sweetly, she again went back over other moments and dwelled especially on that wonderfully soft, innocent caress from that evening on the porch on that first day when he returned to work with Rocky. Methodically, with carefully conditioned strength, she tucked the memories away one by one and then went to the kitchen. The storm was over and the sun was out. As she looked out to the kennel the resolve she had so carefully cultivated over these past months returned and her full strength was restored.

"Out of the frying pan, into the fire," she chuckled to

herself as the old saying flashed across her mind, only to be countered with yet another: "This too will pass."

It was late afternoon before Matt arrived. In a way Irene was surprised to see him, but then again she wasn't. It was more or less consistent with his character as she had come to observe it. She fully expected him to walk in as though absolutely nothing had happened. That's the way he had handled all of their other encounters, always on his terms. This time she was ready for him.

"Hi there," she greeted him warmly. She was an exercise in cheerfulness.

"Hello," he said quietly, obviously puzzled by her demeanor. He had Rocky on a choke leash and was working him in obedience exercises. The dog relaxed from a stiff, alert four-legged stance when he heard Irene's voice and Matt quickly and firmly chastised him. In the show ring lots of people would be milling around and he needed to learn to ignore them, doing only what his handler commanded.

Matt deftly restored Rocky to the proper position and then looked up. Their eyes met and for a moment Irene saw pain and confusion in his, which was not what she expected. She took a deep breath and told herself to be strong. As the silence began to grate, Matt took a deep breath and looked away as he began to address her slowly.

"Look, about last night, well, I understand how you probably feel." His hand went to the back of his neck in a nervous massage. "I was really out of line and, well . . . maybe it would be best if I just take the dog and leave you alone."

"Not on your life!" Irene said firmly. This, she had not expected, but she had come too far down the pike with Rocky and there were still too many inconsistencies for her to relinquish him so easily. "We made a deal," she continued matter-of-factly, "and if you feel you can't continue accordingly, that's your prerogative, but Rocky stays here. The sheriff ruled that he is mine."

For a moment a flash of the old anger returned as Matt's face clouded. He looked at her in calculated silence.

"Now, as for last night," she went on confidently, "really, there is no need to make a big thing out of it. Maybe we both got carried away and . . . sure, I was embarrassed for a moment, but after all I *was* married for two years and I had a wonderful physical relationship with my former husband. It was everything else that didn't work, so as far as I am concerned we should just forget about it. I *know* it won't happen again." Her eyes met his meaningfully, with a hint of challenge. "If you want to go on working the dog," she went on, "I have no quarrel with it—as a matter of-fact, I thought maybe you might help me out. David Thornton has asked me up to his estate, Greentree, Saturday afternoon to show me his dogs and fill me in a little more on their background. You know, of course that he breeds pit bulls. Later we're going to dinner. I thought maybe you might take care of the kennel for me."

Astutely, Irene watched his reaction. To her satisfaction he was patently discomfited, but only for a second. He quickly compensated and answered her with a hearty camaraderie, albeit somewhat forced.

"Sure, be glad to," he said. "And I'm glad there are no hard feelings." Although the inflection of his voice was perfectly controlled his eyes questioned hers and belied a touch of anxiety.

In formulating her survival plan earlier in the morning, Irene had decided that despite some obvious ideological differences, going out with David could prove to be strategically prudent. Although a wise person might have insisted that the best thing was simply to cut the string and send Matt packing, to her that was a cop-out. After all, it was fairly obvious, given her nature, that she might easily be confronted with such a situation again. It was best to face the problem squarely and utilize her inner resources to deal with it and control it, until, just as she had told herself before, Matt's detractions would ultimately render him undesirable. It was just a matter of time. He was most assuredly inappropriate. He had nothing to offer and her common sense would eventually win out.

On the other hand, in retrospect, David had presented some very provocative considerations, and Irene had to admit that her objectivity could easily have been clouded by her emotions reacting to sensational journalism. She was an innately fair person and it really was hard to believe that someone of such obvious refinement and consideration could possibly be involved with something truly heinous. David had a point. Sports were always a contest and danger was often involved. It made little difference if the participants were man or beast.

She had thus justified her decision to utilize this ploy, further bolstered by the fact that apparently the local authorities did not think David was doing anything wrong. As far as she knew, David had never been arrested and everyone was quite aware of his fascination with these dogs. It only followed that others were aware of his involvement in the sport, too.

She simply refused, however, to acknowledge one tiny, deep twinge that insisted something simply did not ring true. Admittedly, David was certainly not the stereotypical character she had most often associated with dog-fighting as she had overheard it discussed in Cedarville, but . . .

"David Thornton. Hmm . . ." Matt said, looking at her

111

speculatively, as he broke into her reflections of the past few seconds, "that's pretty heady company, isn't it?"

Did she actually detect a note of pique? Her strategy was working far better than she had anticipated.

"Yes, he was out the other evening," she responded brightly. "He came again to see Rocky. I'm looking forward to getting away for a while. I didn't realize just how tied down I was, so I really will be appreciative of your help."

"No problem, like I said," he continued. "I'm glad to do it, but from what I hear Thornton's got some pretty interesting hobbies. After the way you've come down on me I have to admit that I'm rather surprised to see that you are involved with him."

For a moment all of her old irritation with his presumptive arrogance surfaced, but she quickly squelched it in accordance with her new resolve.

"Talk is cheap," she said smugly. "David is one of the nicest, most respected men in the area. Of course, he being the intellectual that he is," she continued, "he is also fascinated with the history of the fighting breeds. Chivalry and courage are idealistic standards that he openly admires and he feels a real kinship with his dogs and their history." With that she airily dismissed him and turned to reenter the kennel, but not before she noted, in satisfaction, a distinct note of confusion on his face.

Away from Matt, Irene sat down shakily and wondered openly about this spontaneous, protective deception that had seemed to pour from her vindictively, albeit uncontrollably, when Matt had queried her about her relationship with David. Had she unconsciously aligned herself with all of those others in the community who protected these people even though they, themselves, did not agree with the activity? She wondered, but then, after all, that was the reason she was going out with David—to make up her mind once and for all about this sport.

A few moments later, as she turned from finishing up the paperwork from a newly arrived tenant, Irene glanced through the window and saw Matt as he continued to work with Rocky. He was completely absorbed in the dog's training exercises. Absently she picked up a small Pekingese that scrambled joyously into her arms, and she headed for the empty run she had reserved for it in the kennel. When it was safely situated with its bed and the toys that the owner had brought along, she glanced at the clock and realized she could take a break for an hour or so.

Everything was done in the kennel, but it wasn't yet time for the evening feeding. She had no more sign-ins or pickups scheduled for today. After her fitful night and early-morning rising, along with the attendant tensions that accompanied her anticipation of her meeting with Matt today, she was more than a little tired. A short nap on the deck of the chalet sounded good.

She went out the side entrance of the kennel and circled around, coming into the chalet from the far side so that Matt wouldn't see her as he continued to work on the open lawn between the kennel and the chalet. She had no further wish to have additional contact with him today. Her endurance was already stretched and she could once again feel a familiar pain, as the sight of him wrenched her heart and tried her earlier resolve to "handle" her inappropriate emotions.

She took a quick shower and pulled on loose shorts and halter before settling into a comfortable lounge beneath the warm late afternoon sun. She set a small alarm on the table to remind her of feeding time and opened the novel she had brought along. She found herself unable to concentrate, as Matt's movements faded in and out of her line

113

of vision. Finally, against her better judgment, Irene laid the book aside and allowed herself to watch him in open admiration, secure in the knowledge that he wasn't aware of her presence on the deck.

Matt and the dog seemed to be going through the basic obedience exercises. After Rocky's performance yesterday during the fiasco with Galahad, Irene knew that he was well-versed in these exercises, so this could be little more than a practice session.

She watched in admiration as Matt and the dog took rapid strides across the yard in "precision heeling." Rocky's shoulders were in perfect alignment with Matt's left leg. They looked as though they were a part of a military parade. Matt held the leash loosely but firmly in his right hand. He expertly gave the verbal command to "stay" followed by a resounding "good" as Rocky smoothly and quickly responded.

The sound of Matt's voice so authoritative and manly sent uncontrollable twinges through Irene as she noted the fluid agility of his masculine muscles when he bent to praise the animal. Irene knew she was being foolish, yet somehow she couldn't leave. She continued to watch in fascination.

Matt quickly moved on to the "long down" exercise as with a firm, palm-out hand signal, accompanied by a soft "down," the dog dropped flat on the grass, front feet extended, with his head held proudly alert. Then Matt dropped the leash and stood back about four feet, his arms folded in front of him. He stood like a magnificent statue as the minutes ticked away. Irene could feel herself beginning to drown in unbearable longing. It was another picture she would treasure in the long nights ahead.

Then Matt snapped the silence with an enthusiastic "come" as he continued to the standard "recall" exercise.

Rocky responded immediately to Matt's outstretched hands and Matt was effusive with his petting and praise. Just as quickly he gave the command to "sit" as he dropped the leash after the dog's immediate response and prepared for another four-minute wait during the "long sit" exercise.

Again Matt took up the statue pose and Irene watched in utter enchantment, impervious now to the pain that taunted her and subconsciously urged her to run to him. Finally, just as Irene realized she must make herself leave, they went into the "stand for examination" exercise so extremely important in the show ring.

This was the exercise that allowed the judge to examine the dog carefully while the animal stood in its best form. Slowly Matt brought the dog to "heel" position again as he cautioned him to "stay." He dropped the leash and turned quickly away for just a few seconds before returning to examine the dog by running his hand over his head, back, and hindquarter, ending with his docked tail.

Rocky was superb in his performance and Matt suddenly broke the controlled training atmosphere as he exuberantly shouted, "Good boy! Good boy! You're wonderful!" Then he dropped to the ground in a playful tussle with the dog. Finally, in a fit of enthusiasm, Matt grabbed one of the small, hard rubber dumbbells they had used earlier and flung it twenty feet away while calling loudly, "Go get it, boy, go get it!"

As the dog automatically tore after it Irene was mesmerized by the grace of both the animal and the man. They were truly in accord with one another—a perfect exercise in communication—and they were incredibly beautiful as the red setting sun outlined them in a fiery silhouette.

Irene loved them both, but her feelings for Matt in that

115

instant went far beyond the endurance and limitations of the pain in her heart. She knew she was going to have to learn to live with it, but something told her it was going to be far more difficult than she had anticipated earlier in the day.

CHAPTER EIGHT

Irene dressed carefully for her date with David the next afternoon. She had chosen a dressy culotte that fit her trim figure well. She topped it with a filmy blouse and a lightweight tailored blazer. The day was sunny, but had a hint of nippiness, so she added supple, handmade leather boots to complete the outfit.

She pulled her hair back in a low-riding, sophisticated knot and added jade combs to secure it. Her final touch after again applying skillful makeup that highlighted her eyes and complemented her natural coloring was a pair of chic, simple gold studs that she slipped deftly into her pierced ears. She applied a last dab of fashionable bright lipstick and gave herself a final spray of her favorite cologne. As she observed herself in the mirror she was pleased and felt instantly buoyant and confident.

She went out to give Matt some last-minute instructions. His eyes widened when he saw her and he gave a low macho whistle of appreciation. Irene found it difficult to ignore the giddy feeling his appreciation gave her, all the more disturbing because it was so obviously gauche in expression.

"Please be sure everything is locked up securely," she stated primly, avoiding his gaze, "and be sure the pickup signatures match the sign-in signatures."

"Hey, I did all of this before without any instructions. Remember? Go on and have a good time. I'll take care of everything." His voice was jovial, but his eyes seemed to be veiled, as though his true emotions were being masked. Irene didn't have time, however, to speculate on that observation as David's sleek car pulled up in front of the door.

David was out of the car with a debonair bound and Irene had to admit that he was an extremely handsome, sophisticated man. "How are you, my dear? As always you look wonderful." His gaze passed over her empirically and appreciatively as he stood tapping his keys in his hand.

"Thank you," Irene said rather chastely. "Shall we go, then? I think Matt has everything under control."

"Ah, yes," David said as he recognized Matt, "you were out here the other day. I had no idea that you were working for Irene."

Irene saw a flash of annoyance cross Matt's face, but it was in no way apparent as he responded. "Oh, no, I just give her a hand now and then in return for her boarding my dog." Insolence and mischief. She definitely detected it, but prudently chose to ignore him.

"I understand you are quite a handler of dogs." David looked at Matt meaningfully. "We'll have to get together sometime."

Irene was momentarily stunned, once again thrown off guard and then instantly suspicious. Why would David address Matt in such a way unless he thought he knew something about fighting dogs? This was definitely not a part of her plan. Then, on the other hand, she compensated, David could be referring to the UKC dog-show circuit. He was active in that too. She chastised herself for being too prone to overreaction. In truth she had just about decided that was exactly what she had had, an overreaction. Aside from her now regrettable personal emotions Matt had not given any concrete indication of bad intentions in his work with Rocky. She once again admonished herself to address the real situation at hand—the reality of her feelings for Matt and how to handle them properly.

Within moments they were away and Irene was cradled in the luxury of David's big car, which traveled smoothly over the back roads. She sat back and willed herself to relax and enjoy the freshness of spring that the forest all around them exuded. Soon they came to some low green hills slashed with red clay, where farmers were putting in late crops. A half an hour later they drove through the big gates that announced their arrival at David's ancestral home, Greentree. There was an enormous house at the end of the lane and for a moment Irene felt as though she were in the English countryside rather than the deep South.

"Now that's Carver's Black Boy over there and this sweet lady here is Carver's Tana, all out of the line of Carver."

Irene was standing with David in a well-built kennel area that could easily have rivaled her modest operation. He was enthusiastically introducing her to his favorite animals.

Carver, she thought to herself. *Carver,* there was something familiar about that name.

"Carver, of course," David was lecturing her, "was a legend in his own time. Never been a greater fighting-dog breeder than him and any dog out of his bloodlines is bound to be a noble animal."

The name. The papers, of course. It dawned on Irene

as she silently listened to David, barely paying attention to him. Matt had said one of Rocky's names was Carver!

She felt David take her arm as he carefully began to guide her around the compound. At first glance she had to admit it reminded her of a boxer's training camp—not that she had ever been to one, but it was similar to the ones she had seen portrayed in movies and television.

"It's all a matter of conditioning and training," David was explaining, as he began to point out various pieces of equipment and other paraphernalia used to train the animals. "Now this is a treadmill," he said, pointing to a contraption that was rigged up to allow the dogs to walk or run while staying in the same spot. It had a special harness and something protruding that looked like it might be used to dangle a lure in front of the animal's face, just out of reach.

"Bring Black over here," he called enthusiastically to one of the men who had been hovering nearby. Apparently the man was caretaker of the compound. Within seconds the powerful black dog was comfortably situated in the contraption and obviously impatient to begin the exercise as he danced and whimpered. Saliva began to pour from the dog's mouth as with a yell the handler turned him loose. Within a few seconds Black's legs began to resemble the wheels of a fast-moving locomotive as his ears went back and his mouth parted in a rapidly panting grin. His great teeth gently cradled his tongue, which hung to the side of his mouth as he labored on in outrageous delight.

"Steady boy, steady," David said. "No need to wear that thing out," he laughed. "Now, my dear," he went on, "when you read in those animal welfare rags that the dogs are in combat for hours, well, sometimes they are—rarely much more than an hour though—but as you can see they are conditioned for it. Black, here, could go at controlled paces for hours on the treadmill and he obviously loves it. He instinctively realizes he is fulfilling his destiny."

An instinctive concern, the warning that indicates when one is in the presence of fanaticism, went off resoundingly in Irene's subconscious. She looked at David quietly and realized innately that here was a man completely enthralled with some sort of fantasy that he had embellished with medieval mores.

As the handler slowed the dog down the conditioned muscular strength of the animal was almost awesome. He was beautiful and exciting in the most dangerous sense of the word.

As David continued to guide her around with his hand protectively on her elbow, Irene began to feel decidedly uncomfortable with his nearness and assumed familiarity. She noticed that the animals were housed in specially constructed runs that utilized wood and chain-link fence. There were about thirty of them in the compound. They had special resting platforms and snug houses. Apparently the dogs spent their entire lives outdoors, which was, of course, perfectly acceptable when they were provided for in this manner. The entire run was elevated, with a screen of fence extending from the platform and a smooth concrete slab beneath that was easily cleaned. It was a very impressive and efficient arrangement—not at all the way Irene had pictured their care from what she had read. Each run was equipped with stainless steel utensils, and an air of cleanliness and concern prevaded the entire area.

"As you can see, every precaution is taken to protect the health of the dogs, and the 'keep,' or diet, of each one is scientifically regulated to insure that they are in top condition," explained David.

Irene had to admit that she had never seen a happier or better-kept group of animals. All of this had to cost a fortune—she could just imagine the vet bills alone—but then David apparently had the money to spend and this was his hobby.

"Now, every animal you have just seen has been in combat," David said as he astutely gauged her reaction, "and as you can see, none of them has been seriously injured. To be sure," he continued expansively, "they have had bruises and lacerations, but they healed. All of them are champions or out of champions," he ended proudly. "I never allow anything but champions in my pack."

His last words sent a chill through Irene. She wondered what a loser looked like. She understood that they were an embarrassment to their owners, and from the way David obviously identified with his animals she could understand why, but naggingly she wondered what their condition was before they were destroyed.

"Is there no way," she said, deliberately baiting him, "that a truly brave, or as you define it, game dog can lose and still maintain its dignity, its right to exist? Are there not instances when an animal is simply mismatched, but nevertheless brave enough to battle?"

"My dear, you continue to insist upon clouding this with emotion, and your, forgive me, ignorance is once again apparent." David looked at her with a tender, indulgent air. "To answer your first question, most assuredly yes. I told you we are not barbarians. The object of our sport is very simply to test the braveness of the animals, not to kill or injure them. As you know, most canines instinctively submit when they know they are beaten. That is the natural law of the pack and assures the survival of the fittest. When, however, these dogs have been truly bred they are endowed with such a supreme self-confidence that they simply do not acknowledge such a trait. The only time an owner can possibly be embarrassed by one of these animals is when someone has desecrated the bloodlines and the dog turns tail and runs. That, my dear, is a cur and not to be tolerated. For the sake of the breed they must be destroyed, but I daresay," he continued, as he noted the concern on her face, "that is certainly no worse than the millions of animals killed in humane society shelters each year—and they have the gall to condemn us." He sniffed contemptuously.

"But to finish answering your question, we have very precise rules with safeguards that allow any handler to 'pickup' his dog, or concede, anytime he wishes, if he sees that an otherwise game dog is just off its pace or in some other way momentarily impaired, and there is no disgrace in that—of course, it's not good for the reputation of the dog, but it's no disgrace either . . . just good sense in some instances." His face reflected obvious distaste as he spoke the last words. "And then occasionally," he went on as they began to leave the compound, "you have an animal genuinely, grievously injured, which in good conscience you may think you just can't allow to go on, but it's just raring to go back. Dogs such as this have been known to come back and win, only to die afterward, but to have stopped the animal, in that supreme moment, would have broken its spirit and robbed it of its rightful glory."

Irene looked at him in absolute amazement. David really was in another world. *Whose glory?* her conscience nagged inwardly. She recalled a line from the movie *Patton:* "His guts, our blood."

As they neared the perimeter of the compound, three or four large pit bulls not as conditioned as those Irene had just seen were staked at strategic intervals, and they began to set off an unholy racket.

"Now, these," David said gesturing to them, "just to show you that we are not beasts, are competitors that did not quite make the grade. They serve now as lookouts and 'roll' dogs, or sparring partners, when we are training the others, and as you can readily see, they too, are healthy and happy."

Again Irene had to admit that what David was saying was most apparent. The dogs stood wide-legged and alert, tails wagging furiously as they fulfilled their appointed duties. As Irene watched them she was mesmerized by the sweeping action of their long, sturdy tails and then a dark, sick lump suddenly thumped in her stomach. She hadn't noticed it before.

"David, don't you routinely dock the tails of your dogs? Doesn't that make them strategically better fighters?"

"Oh, my dear, no. I never do," he said almost impatiently. "I show some of my dogs and UKC doesn't allow docked tails in their standards. Now some of the amateurs are doing it . . ." he went on, but Irene didn't hear him.

Rocky's tail was docked. There was no way he could be shown in the upcoming UKC show. He had lied to her. Matt Davis had lied to her from the beginning! All of her original suspicions had been correct.

In confusion Irene realized that David was still talking to her. "And to answer your last question, the dogs are never mismatched. A 'contract' is always made beforehand and the precise weight of the animals is stipulated . . ."

Before he could finish, Irene broke in, interrupting him rudely. "Rocky has a docked tail! He has a docked tail!" she said again in obvious agitation. "There is no way he can be shown in the UKC show."

"I daresay not," said David, startled by her unexpected outburst. "It sounds as though your friend Matt Davis has been, shall we say, feeding you a line. Tell me, my dear," he said somewhat conspiratorially, "just how did you manage to get yourself involved with this fellow in the first place? Did you not say you had some argument or something over the dog . . . or something, just what was it?"

"I found Rocky," Irene said in a distressed voice, "and, well, I thought he was being groomed for the dogfight pit and after all that I had heard I just didn't want to see that happen to him. When Matt tried to claim him I wouldn't give him up. I'd gotten his tags and the sheriff backed me up."

"It went that far," David said in amazement, "and the sheriff backed you against him?"

"Yes, and then, well . . . Matt came around and apologized and insisted that he had bought Rocky to show him in the UKC show and well . . . I guess I felt guilty and wanted to believe him; but there's been something funny about this right from the beginning."

"As I told you," David said indulgently, "a great deal of riffraff has been attracted to our sport. They have no idea about proper conditioning or ethics . . . I daresay if your original suspicions were correct, your concern for the animal was well-founded. From what I've seen of the dog he has been botched by an amateur, first the ears and then the tail, and his spirit seemed mediocre at best the other evening."

Irene inwardly cringed at the last statement and to her amazement felt a small note of resentment. She had seen Rocky's potential, and then she quickly realized that she was beginning to think the same as a dogfighter. Rocky's most winning qualities were not his aggressivness, but his gentleness, his comedy. That's what had drawn her to him in the first place.

"Oh, I do apologize, Irene, that was extremely insensitive of me." David was sincerely contrite. "I know how devoted you are to that animal and he truly has some fine qualities, but I honestly do not think he is suited for combat. I have one in the house, Lady, who is ages old now, just like him. She was one of my first dogs, but she was never meant to be more than a pet. She's been my one weakness and I keep her completely away from my other stock."

Irene was in a daze as they continued on into David's palatial home. "You know, though, I have heard talk about this fellow, Davis. Seems he has been making the rounds of the fighting circles and from what everyone says he seems to be a natural handler."

Irene was sure she was going to faint. She looked for a chair and gratefully sank into it as David continued, glad that he didn't notice her discomfiture. "But they have all been a little leery of him. We have to be careful of 'snitches,' you know. Those big, slick animal welfare groups are always trying to infiltrate, but if you say the sheriff would have nothing to do with his claim, Davis must be clean. The sheriff is beginning to prove himself somewhat of an irritant lately—what with the booze and drugs the riffraff bring in he's beginning to get some pressure, but nothing that we can't handle," he mused. "I can always use a good hand," David said, looking at her meaningfully. "Maybe with a little guidance Davis can be nudged in the right direction and you won't need to worry about your Rocky." He smiled at her, ever indulgent.

She was in a bad dream. This *had* to be a bad dream. David was obviously incapable of comprehending the reality of his world, or he simply did not wish to. Matt, with all of his lies, was obviously even worse and she, fool that she was, had fallen in love with him. . . . It was a nightmare completely out of control. Irene prayed that morning consciousness would soon arrive and bring it to an end. Little did she know that her anguish and suffering had only begun.

It was later in the evening and David and Irene had retired to his library, which was dark, warm, and wooden in the manner of any estate house built early in the cen-

126

tury. She was sipping a sherry and trying to talk with him companionably. In her agitated and bewildered state earlier in the afternoon she had not felt up to going out to a restaurant, so David had very quickly ordered an elegant, light meal, which his cook had no problem in producing in a relatively short time.

It had been ages since Irene had had fresh artichokes, and the small steaks broiled to perfection capped with giant whole mushrooms had been delicious. A delectable salad and a finale of exquisite fruit and cheese topped off now with this wonderful cream sherry had done much to restore her spirits.

In her usual manner Irene realized she was probably once again a victim of her own overworked imagination, which ultimately resulted in an acute overreaction. She had to admit that she had not really seen anything bad this afternoon. On the contrary, what she had seen was some magnificent animals being treated as though they were in the Taj Mahal. Her confusion over Matt Davis was an entirely different matter, but it should not have been unexpected. She would take care of that tomorrow morning. She intended to send him packing more for his deceit now than his obvious ulterior motives throughout this charade.

"You see, my dear," David said, ever solicitous and considerate as he cut the tip from an expensive, slim cigar, "these animals are truly magnificent and are rarely harmed—no more than any other properly conditioned athlete, when they are handled properly. This is precisely the standard that I wish to reestablish by making this sport legitimate."

Irene had mellowed out considerably since the afternoon and she had managed to almost entirely submerge her nagging doubts.

"But, David, don't you honestly worry about being involved in something where you might be arrested or

. . ." Her voice trailed off as her eyes questioned him in concern.

"Oh my, no," he said in perfect confidence. "To begin with, my hobby has as much to do with the actual conditioning and development of the animals as with the battle. I never handle the dogs myself—I pay handsomely for the best handlers that money can buy and their loyalty to me is unquestioned. It is certainly not illegal to own these animals or to train and condition them, at least not in most places. Should, most unfortunately, a match or 'convention,' which is a series of matches, be raided, although it is a first degree misdemeanor in many places to be a spectator, with a fine of five hundred dollars or more, I can assure you that no judge from around here would ever adjudicate me, although I doubt if the district attorney's office would even bother to press charges, so it would never get that far." He smiled at her rather smugly. "I am a lawyer, you know," he said in a low voice. "You can be sure I have all of the bases covered, but I can also assure you that the possibility of a raid ever being conducted in this area is extremely remote. We are very close-knit. We don't allow just anyone to participate and once the fight begins no one can leave."

Once again a little nagging twinge began to bother Irene. She heard the telephone ring and the butler appeared shortly to summon David to it. Left alone in the room she began to wander about, glancing over the books and magazines strewn about. Idly she picked up something that looked like a badly put together bulletin of some kind. The words *Pit Dog Report* were emblazoned across the cover.

Instantly curious, she began to leaf through it and was almost immediately appalled by the pictures and incredibly bad writing, which resembled backwoods colloquial language at its very worst. There were pages and pages of blow-by-blow accounts of dogs in battle, graphic enough to chill the marrow in her bones. Shakily she turned a few more pages and noticed some amateur "how to" articles with reference to training and conditioning, multitudes of ads advertising puppies and stud service, and finally maudlin, preachy pieces that were indicative of much infighting and recognition that some among them needed to clean up their act, as the presence of drugs and boorish manners were openly decried as harmful to the sport.

Irene could not for the life of her imagine David being involved with such people, with all of his pretentious airs. He was obviously operating on an entirely different plane, far removed from reality. As she turned to the last page she came upon a poem apparently penned by one of the revered old-timers of the sport who had recently passed on. She began to read in an almost bewitched fascination:

A Pit Bull Dog, Or a Game Cock
Fight From a Hatred Too Deep
   For Man To Understand
Except On Those Night Of
The Soul When We Touch The
Blackness That Lie Buried
Within Us All. They Fight
For Vendetta That Was Old
When Man Was Young. For a
Slight Incurred In Some
Prehistoric Place a
Millennion Ago. They
   Fight
Because It Is Ther
   Destiny.
To Die Game,
   By Me.

* * *

129

It was an obvious photocopy of a handwritten sheet and the lines were shaky and uneven. It was without a doubt the most singularly revealing, intuitive thing she had ever read. Although this was a crude version of David's favorite defense and justification of this activity, Irene was shocked and astounded by the arrogance of this simplistic assumption as portrayed through the starkness and bluntness of these broken words.

"Colorful characters, aren't they?" David had reentered the room and saw Irene with the magazine in her hand. "You know, when you start dealing with 'folks' you have to take everything with a grain of salt. When I reach my objective these dogs will be restored to their rightful place among kings and queens, heads of state, and they will be written about in slick glossy magazines, and the dignity that they deserve, that they once had, will be theirs again."

His eyes always took on a fervent gleam when he began to talk this way and again Irene found it hard to reconcile his role and belief with the facts, which were readily apparent.

"David," she said plaintively, "have you and the others who think the way you do ever considered, since your entire interest is in demonstrating the gameness of the dogs, providing them with some sort of protective paraphernalia, some padding, the same as they do for football players and boxers and all of the others? It seems that truly the only objection, and justifiably so, is to the injuries the dogs sustain."

"Oh, my dear, naive, sweet thing," he said, looking at her enticingly, "you are precious, you're wonderful, fiery and brave, and I'd love to be with you when you have finally witnessed a truly noble battle between these dogs. I'm sure your expression would be wonderful to behold." He stepped closer to her and now he began to twine his

130

hand through her hair, releasing it from the combs as he pulled her to him and began to gently nuzzle and caress her lovely neck. "Then you would see," he went on huskily, between caresses, "just how preposterous such a suggestion is."

Irene stood numbly, riveted to the spot, unable to will herself to rebuff him. Slowly, he set down his glass and cigar and then encircled her in his arms in a gentle embrace. "You are lovely," he said "and we must get to know one another well."

His voice was gentle and sweet, his caresses only mildly demanding and suggestive, the exact opposite of those she had experienced with Matt Davis; but somehow they were filled with a menace that sent terrifying chills throughout her body. She could sense a subliminal condescension that seemed to strip her bare, destroying her dignity, and she fought valiantly to suppress her true emotions.

Secretly she was a little afraid of him and she wished now only to return back to her safe, secure abode in the chalet. She had been on the emotional seesaw long enough and now it was time to take matters into her own hands.

"You're kind, David," she murmured in her most convincing, chaste voice, "but I'm really very tired and I think it would be best if I were to return home. I have a big day tomorrow."

"By all means," he said smoothly, as he stepped lightly away. "I thought perhaps you might enjoy coming out again tomorrow evening when we will have a little more action than what we had today."

Irene looked at him momentarily dumbfounded. Seeing her reaction, he spoke hastily to reassure her. "No, no, my dear, we are not having a match, but we have arranged to roll a few of the better local competitors—you know, somewhat of a sparring contest in which the animals are not allowed to actually engage other than a few 'hits,' or

131

swipes, in preparation for arranging contracts for the big convention coming down late this summer. I'm sure you would find it enlightening, not to mention . . ." he said speculatively, "exciting."

Bewildered, Irene was speechless, as a silly smile that David mistook for interest illuminated her face.

"Some of those colorful characters you have been reading about in that book will be here, too, and I'm sure you, with all of your sophistication, will find the whole thing rather amusing."

Unable to think of anything that would not offend him, Irene nodded in numb assent and went hurriedly to gather up her purse so he could take her home.

CHAPTER NINE

Irene was up early the next morning, in a raging torrent of emotions. Matt had been gone when she arrived home the evening before and David had left her graciously, without any further attempts at intimacies. She dressed hurriedly in trim jeans and a tight-fitting blouse and went directly to the kennel lobby. Angrily she rummaged through the papers in the desk until she found the UKC standards that Matt had given her a few days before. She quickly scanned them until her eyes fell at last on the incriminating information tucked away in the middle of the page in small print. She read it rapidly. There were no exceptions. Docked or bobbed tails were not acceptable for American pit bull terriers.

That liar! She hurled the paper across the room in outrage. That lying scum. He had been playing her for the fool of the century and she, like an idiotic schoolgirl, had let him take her in. She had refused to listen to her own intuitive common sense and warnings so she could indulge in her primitive physical passions. Well, no more!

Almost as if on cue, Matt's truck pulled up outside. He

stepped jovially through the door, but one look at Irene's face told him this was the end.

"You lying heel," she said in deadly tones. "You liar! You can't show Rocky in the UKC show," she shouted as she retrieved the paper and flung it toward him. "UKC does *not* allow docked or bobbed tails! This whole thing has been a sham from the beginning and you have had nothing but debased, primitive intentions for that dog from the beginning."

Seeing that she was completely beyond reason, Matt made no effort to appease her. "Why in the hell are you coming down so hard on me?" His eyes flashed and bore into her face like pistol shots. "You know you haven't been exactly subtle with your insinuations." The derision in his voice was a study in condescension. He looked at her with genuine distaste while she stood numbly, unable to speak now that she had spent her emotional charge.

She was weary of the battle and just wanted it to end. After learning what she had at David's house last night there was no doubt in her mind. No one else would do it. No one else cared, so it was up to her. Somehow she had to do something to get this terrible practice stopped and that meant remaining for the time being in David's good graces. She couldn't do that and continue this constant emotional conflagration and uncertainty that Matt's presence constantly provoked. She had no time now to consider his peripheral role, David was the one she needed to concentrate on.

"That rich bastard you're pussyfooting around with has probably killed and maimed thousands of dogs just like Rocky . . ." The sneer in his voice died to an uneasy silence as Matt suddenly took on an air of obvious discomfiture, almost as if he had spoken out of turn.

Irene looked at him with a puzzled expression, but she really had no time to dwell on his obvious Jekyll-Hyde syndrome now. "Your opinion is of *no* interest to me," she said in a deadly monotone. "I want you to leave and I *never* want to see you around here again."

The stillness was suffocating as their eyes locked in an empty eternity. The pain that was screaming through Irene was mercifully numbed by the horror she had at last fully comprehended. Without her protection Rocky would have surely been ripped to shreds by animals such as those she had just seen the evening before.

Slowly Matt began to move. He looked for his hat, which he had flung away in frustration during their shouting match. His angry eyes were shrouded in a plea for understanding, which in her present state Irene was incapable of comprehending. She turned to leave, but suddenly he was across the room and his strong arms were circling her in a rough, urgent embrace. Before she could squirm away his lips came crushing down on hers, hard and cruel, sensuously demanding. Then, in almost contemptuous disgust, he flung her away from him.

Irene stumbled and fell against the wall in dazed shock. Breathing heavily, Matt said with a sneer, "You can consider that my official good-bye, but before I go let me give you one last piece of advice. Stay out of things you don't know anything about. People can get hurt that way!"

The echo of the door slamming reverberated through Irene's soul and took up residence with the rest of her bruised and aching memories. Had he actually threatened her? As she began to recover, the implications of his words began to sink in. Was he actually implying that she was in danger if she didn't back off?

Suddenly the room took on a distinct chill, in direct contradiction to the warmth of the day. Painfully Irene massaged her arms and began to brush her disheveled hair back, but her long fingers compellingly hovered near her lips, which were still tingling from that vicious embrace:

stinging and cruel, it nevertheless had evoked a provocative and disturbing response. . . .

Then, resolutely, in conformance with her conditioning, she stood up straight and brushed herself off as her dignity slowly returned. She had things to do. She had to be ready to meet David again and he had to believe he had won her completely.

The terms were guttural and violent and seemed to have sadistic, sexual connotations as the men's voices lowered and the women squirmed in anticipation. Irene was at David's estate again and she was witnessing for the first time the rolling of dogs. Earlier in the evening there had been a delicious barbecue and there was plenty of beer for everyone. Children played in the distance, although an equal number were right here, deeply engrossed in the violence that even quasi-confrontations provided.

While Irene was feeling a distinct sense of revulsion, from the corner of her eye she saw hands beginning to wander unconsciously in erotic trails as couples began to move closer together in unison with the overall frenzy of the dogs straining at their leashes, anxious for battle.

"Damn, they're ready," said one man in abandoned anticipation. He was in a half-crouch and his hand moved unconsciously to adjust his trousers through the crotch as he leered expectantly at the animals. "That fast mouth Black is ready to tear that rough red nose Gator to bits. Let 'em hit one, just once," he begged, as his eyes took on a wild look.

The terms the man had used were references to the biting techniques and breeding of the animals involved. Irene was rapidly picking up a whole new glossary of terminology that characterized dogfighting and was an indication of who was in the know and who was not—a useful tool in flushing out snitches.

136

"No, those are two of my best studs," David said meaningfully to the man. "I don't want them touching each other. Let them save it for the pit. When the big convention comes down in August, just remember what you've seen, unless, of course someone here wants to work up a contract tonight."

"Thornton?" said one of the men quizzically, while looking meaningfully at Irene.

"Oh, don't worry about Irene, here," David said, comprehending the man's question.

David had maintained a general air of superiority throughout the evening, but the people there, far from being offended, seemed to almost pay him homage.

"She's one of us," he went on. "She's got a dog of her own and a growing boarding kennel business down south." He glanced at Irene pointedly as his fingers lightly tousled her hair and suggestively outlined her ear. "Irene's an intelligent woman who wants to get the true picture," he ended affectionately.

In confusion, Irene smiled at him brightly, terrified that her true emotions might, in some way, be apparent. Somehow she managed to get through the rest of the evening, which thankfully consisted of only a few hits. When David brought her home at last, he again left her with only a perfunctory good-night kiss, which was more of a meaningless gesture than a caress. His eyes, however, told her that he was waiting, patiently waiting, and he knew it would be worth it.

Going into the house, Irene immediately sensed that something was wrong. Buffy came bounding out, barking up his usual storm of greeting, dancing all about in gleeful anticipation, but he was alone.

She understood immediately what had happened. Rocky was gone and she knew who had him. Frantically, she went from room to room, but it was no use. She knew the dog was nowhere to be found and the house was eerily empty without him. She looked at her watch. It was well past midnight. Common sense told her that it was best to wait until morning. Wearily she made her way to bed where she spent another restless, fitful night.

Irene was at the sheriff's office bright and early the next morning, pounding on the door. She was soon to learn, to her ultimate despair, that the ally she had counted on in that office no longer existed.

"Woman, I don't know what you expect of me," the sheriff boomed as he blustered about the office with a steaming coffee mug in his hand. "I've done all I can for you. I ruled in your favor once and then you let Davis come back and practically move in. His claim to the dog is, to be honest, just as legit as yours and we both knew that from the beginning. You have only yourself to blame for this."

He thumped the mug down on the desk and sat down in his chair with an exasperated sigh before he went on. "For that matter you don't have any proof that Davis even has the dog. From what you've told me a dog disappeared just a few hours ago. You'll just have to understand, Miss Malone," he ended in an expansive dismissal, "I've got a whole county of people to take care of. I don't have time to worry about animals too!"

Irene knew as her heart sank that it would do no good to attempt to discuss her suspicions, let alone mention anything about David Thornton. The sheriff was probably one of "them" too and to tip her hand to him now would most assuredly label her as a snitch, and her chances of ending the dogfighting in this area would most certainly go down the drain.

No, she was on her own. She would have to find another way. For the moment, however, she had to find Rocky.

After what David had told her about Matt's contacts in the area there was no doubt that her original suspicions were true and he planned to put Rocky in the dogfighting pit.

Thinking back now, she remembered once again the cat incident and the scene when Rocky tore the pillow to bits. She wondered now what used to take place in the woods when Matt and the dog went for long jaunts—come to think of it, running had been an integral part of Matt's contact with Rocky. That would be one way of accomplishing what a treadmill ordinarily would have if the trainer were set up more formally.

Other memories insidiously began to creep in also. Irene's throat tightened and she began to find it difficult to breathe as she remembered his smiling eyes, that stubborn tendril of hair, forever falling from his dark widow's peak, his hands as they whispered over her, awakening responses she had never known she had, and lastly, never to be forgotten, his kisses, sweet and gentle, hard and demanding, his twinkling eyes and mischievous banter . . .

Was there to be no mercy? He had now proven himself to be akin to the lowest vermin on the earth, and God help her, she still loved him—not only loved him, but wanted him and needed him.

Feeling the tears welling up behind her eyes, Irene turned from the sheriff. She ran from the office and struggled blindly with the door handle on her car. She didn't see the troubled, deep concern in the sheriff's eyes as she went through the door. She had only the memory of his derision and lack of concern.

The chancre of the area was now contaminating her entire existence and breaking her heart beyond repair. The only salvation she could possibly have was the finding of Rocky before some great harm befell him. To do that she had to find Matt Davis and forget forever her feelings about him. Recalling the touches of David and her growing involvement with him, she inwardly shuddered. She realized that she was probably going to have to endure much more if she were to succeed in her quest to stop the dogfight. Her conflicts with these two men mingled so incompatibly with her personal ethics that she was left in a constant state of frustration. Her peaceful existence was rapidly becoming a living hell.

She pulled into her drive with a heavy heart and was again instantly reminded of Rocky's absence. It was a special silence that pervaded over all of the other commotion. Once again her resolve strengthened as she went into the house. To succeed, Irene realized that she must formulate a logical, realistic plan. One that she, alone, could execute.

CHAPTER TEN

It was as though he had disappeared from the face of the earth. It had been four months now since the disappearance of Rocky, and Irene had been unable to locate even the slightest trace of information. Too late, she had realized that she knew absolutely nothing about Matt Davis. She had never heard him mention the name of his employer, she had no address of the motel where he had said he was staying—not even a telephone number.

Oh, she had been easy, all right. He had just shown up like some phantom and she had been so enthralled with controlling her sophomoric responses that she had not learned even the merest basic facts about him and in return she had practically given him the run of her place. It was impossible to count the number of agonizing moments she had expended berating herself and trying unsuccessfully to purge him from her heart.

David had shown her the greatest sympathy and consideration. In a magnanimous gesture he tried to extend his influence to assist in finding the dog, but all to no avail. Irene had continued to see him on a very regular basis and in the process allowed him to assume a rather proprietary air about her, thankful that his fascination was further whetted and encouraged by her natural reserve.

David's intentions were fairly obvious, but in the course of these few months it had become clear to Irene that he derived his most supreme satisfaction from a mingled sense of stalking and violence. It was like a big game to him. In love, as with everything else, he needed to wax supreme, and ultimately his quarry must be vanquished and ravished, after which it would simply be tossed aside.

She was walking a dangerous emotional tightrope, but she knew she had to hang in until she had something concrete to offer the federal authorities. That was her only hope now, for as David had so deftly pointed out, he was not breaking any laws. Unless an actual dogfight were in process there was really very little anyone could do.

During the past months Irene had witnessed many more evenings when dogs were rolled. She had little more to go on than that a major dogfight convention was coming down at about the same time as the UKC dog show— another indication of David's craftiness. A large number of pit bull fanciers would be expected in the area at that time as well as those who insisted they used these dogs for hunting and nothing more. They were always around looking for good puppies at bargain prices.

Matt seemed to have literally disappeared too, making only cursory appearances in the area. Irene had not been able to track him down . . . until now.

She was sitting in dark shadows, watching from her car, as the noisy, discordant notes of the honky-tonk bar across the way drifted through the night. It had been hours, but she knew he was in there.

Her young kennel helper, Jeff, had called her earlier in the evening and told her he had spotted Matt's truck in town, and someone else had seen Lola. In the past weeks she had made it her business to learn all about the local hangouts where the dogfighters usually congregated. Once she had actually been brave enough to go into one, but she had soon conceded that there were still places where it definitely was not safe for a woman to enter alone unless she was looking for what leering glances and suggestive greeting promised.

It had been a simple process of elimination before Irene finally found the big truck. She had stealthily crept around it and found telltale evidence in the nature of heavy collars, leashes, break sticks, and other paraphernalia that indicated someone was working with a dog. Many showed traces of white hair and once again she had to stifle the pain that shot through her. She dared not to think of what they may have turned Rocky into. For the moment she cared only about getting him back.

As the minutes ticked on Irene once again recalled Matt's words on that fateful day when Lola came to pick him up the first time. "It's not what you think. This whole thing is not what you think." His words had become a nagging refrain that she derisively answered over and over again, "You can say that again." Never in her wildest dreams, after all of her conditioning and attempts at worldliness, would she have believed she could have been so gullible. Matt had practically mapped out his entire plan and she had been too stupid to see it and in the process had fallen in love with him too. "Oh, how he must enjoy himself. He and Lola probably laugh about it every night!" she fumed to herself.

Suddenly the door from the tavern opened and the light split the darkness of the night, illuminating Matt and Lola as they practically tumbled through it with arms awkwardly entwined about each other, while their high-pitched, boisterous laughter echoed through the darkness. In obvious drunken banter Irene heard Matt call out, "See

143

you guys later. We'll take care of that business next week," as they stumbled on to the truck.

Instantly alert, Irene waited until they had started the truck and then she began to follow them furtively. She had to learn where they were staying. From that maybe she could get a lead on Rocky. Slowly and then much more rapidly she followed the truck through the now deserted streets. She couldn't believe how competently Matt was driving the truck. Both he and Lola had straightened up and seemed to be talking animatedly. Before long they came to some of the better beachfront motels in the area and to Irene's surprise Matt pulled into one of them. "Cheap motel," she said out loud. "No wonder I've been having trouble. I even believed that."

There was a wonderful stretch of white beach that would have been perfect for running a dog and Irene noted that animals were allowed. She tried to stay back until she could see what room Matt and Lola went into—there was no doubt in her mind that they were both going into the same room. As soon as she could, without being detected, she had to get close enough to see if Rocky was there.

She watched carefully as they continued to talk and then entered a door on the parking lot side. She saw no hint of a commotion, which would indicate the dog's presence. The lights went on in the room. Somehow she couldn't compel herself to leave, even though there was probably nothing more she could learn that night.

The lights continued to stay on and Irene thought she detected further hints of laughter followed by short silences; silences long enough for caresses and the first teasing stages of familiar lovemaking. Realizing that she was probably worse than a common voyeur, she continued to watch as room service delivered beer and sandwiches. It was almost as if she were willing herself to stay and watch as a punishment for her own inadequacies.

About thirty minutes later Irene saw the lights go out and once again the pain she had endured for so long during that "other" time, long before the advent of Matt, came cascading back, completely immobilizing her. Blinded by hot tears she groped for the ignition and failed to see the handsome, dark-haired man in the sleek, sporty car that suddenly pulled away from the building and zoomed noisily down the road. With a heavy sigh she turned toward home, trying to think what her next maneuver should be.

A few days later Irene sat on her couch in complete despair. Afraid that she might be noticed she had solicited the help of Jeff and some of his friends to watch the movements of Matt and Lola. Her preoccupation with this problem was also beginning to have detrimental effects on her business, so she dared not risk any further neglect by leaving her responsibilities in the hands of others too often. Jeff and his friends had failed to uncover even the slightest additional clue. Although both Lola and Matt were seen often in the dogfighter hangouts, Jeff and the others had never once seen Rocky or any sign that he was in Matt's possession. Apparently Matt had him hidden away somewhere and Irene was simply not in a position to do much more about it.

Common sense told her that it was time to begin putting the pieces of her life together again. It was also becoming increasingly clear that her objectives with reference to David Thornton were rather naive too. He was a rich and powerful man. Her continued plan to interfere with his passionate interest in dogfighting would probably ultimately do little more than ruin her. She would lose everything she had worked so hard to achieve. She was a grown woman and it was a cruel world. The fate of one dog like Rocky and the activities of all the Davids in the world

were really nothing compared to other worldwide trage-
dies and travesties. She was foolish to think she could
accomplish anything alone and it was perfectly plain that
she could expect no help from the local authorities.

With a sigh she arose and went out on the porch. The
house was still empty and lonely in spite of the animated
antics that Buffy continued to exhibit as he cavorted
around in perpetual glee.

"May as well begin somewhere," she said out loud to
herself in resignation as she began to finger the ruins of the
macrame hangers that Rocky had destroyed. She had
never gotten around to removing them, let alone replacing
them. For that matter she had allowed many other things
to slide, and her home and personal appearance were beginning to take on a rather unkempt appearance, which
was completely out of character for her.

Realizing that she was about to be overtaken with a
debilitating depression if she did not take positive steps to
counter it, Irene returned inside and rummaged through
her storeroom until she found the materials she needed to
replace the hangers. Working with her hands had always
proven therapeutic and now she looked forward to the
activity.

She bent to give Buffy a playful pat and realized that she
had also been neglecting him. Somehow now it was almost
painful to tussle with him and chatter to him as she went
about her chores because it reminded her so much of the
time spent with Rocky. "But that's not your fault, is it?"
she said. The little dog was almost delirious with delight.
He had practically worn himself out during the past few
months trying to regain her attention.

As she went past the mirror, Irene realized painfully
that her appearance was almost haggard and, in fact, it
had been more than a week since David had called. Not
that she really cared. Certainly that was a relationship she

was going to sever in any event, but it bothered her to think that she was letting herself go to the point of no longer being attractive. It was bad enough that she had made a complete fool of herself over Matt Davis, she didn't need to put herself on the shelf permanently. As soon as she got the hanger going, she made a mental note to treat herself to a hot tub and general all-over beauty treatment.

Looking at her hands, she realized ruefully that it had been weeks since she had done her nails. One of her strictest personal requirements in the past had been making sure she gave herself a manicure once a week, utilizing clear, natural polish to prevent her hands from growing rough and unladylike from her work in the kennel. They were in sad, sad shape now. Looking at the clock, she decided that although it was midday her opening revitalization thrust would be better spent in getting herself back into shape. Quickly she carried the macrame twine to the porch along with her tape measure and scissors and then returned to enjoy a wonderfully long, relaxing soak.

She had just completed the final touches on her nails while she luxuriated in a silky, filmy caftan when the phone rang. Quickly setting the manicure utensils aside, she went to answer the phone. She gasped when she heard the voice on the other end, but only in shock. It no longer had the power to upset her. It was her former husband.

"Jerry, what on earth do you want?" she asked matter-of-factly. One thing Irene did not need was any further complications in her life at this moment, but she found curiously that her response to him was little more than a polite interest, which she might have had for a long lost acquaintance or college chum who suddenly turned up.

"I was just in the area," she heard him say as she came out of her momentary preoccupation. "Well, not really in the area," he continued, "unless you can call seventy-five

147

miles in the area." He gave a little laugh as though encouraging her to join him in his little joke. She remained silent, trying to decide her response in anticipation of what she knew was coming. Actually, she had more or less expected this to happen sooner or later, but this definitely was not the time. Jerry apparently sensed her attitude, as his voice took on a slightly nervous tinge.

"I know we have nothing more to say to each other," he plunged right in, "but there is a little legal matter that was somehow neglected when we made our property agreements and I need to discuss it with you to just tidy everything up."

Tidy everything up. How like him. Yet she really didn't feel the impatience she was trying to impart. "And what could that be?" she asked, honestly curious now. She was under the impression that everything was settled.

"Well," he said with a rather contrived charm, "remember the contract we had signed to buy a vacation condo that had just begun construction and wasn't slated to be finished for two years?"

"Yes . . . yes." She did remember and it had completely slipped her mind.

"Well, I'd like to go ahead and complete the sale," Jerry went on, "but the original contract was in both of our names, so I need to have you sign a waiver and I'll return half of the deposit to you. I would have just sent it through a lawyer," he continued, "but after all of this time I thought maybe both of us had paid out more than enough to those guys and I had to come your way anyway. Is there any chance we could get together, over dinner perhaps, and take care of this without a hassle?"

No, there really wasn't any reason why not. Although she had no real desire to see him, Irene had to admit that there was still a little satisfaction in hearing from Jerry in this manner. She had no axes to grind and she had no

148

interest in the condo now, so his offer was more than reasonable. Unless, of course, her astute business mind suddenly flashed, Jerry was thinking of reselling it and making a handsome profit. Real estate had escalated outrageously during the past two years. Maybe it would be better to offer to sell him her half. The thought of that was suddenly very gratifying and in view of the events of the past few weeks just the type of thing she needed to restore her confidence.

"What did you have in mind?" she asked at last.

"Well, I can come over there . . . or"—he paused, not hearing ready assent from her—"you can come over here. I'm in Harborville and there is a wonderful restaurant right on the water."

Instinctively Irene did not in any way relish the idea of his coming there and in any way besmirching her lair. She had created it completely away from his influence and somehow the thought of him in *her* chalet was disturbing. No, neutral ground would be better, and considering everything, a long drive and new scenery might be just the ticket to complete her rejuvenation. Quickly she made the arrangements to meet him the next evening and hung up the phone feeling very smug with herself.

Already feeling much better she made a light pirouette around the room and went out to begin the macrame hanger. She had just gotten the long eight-foot strands of twine measured and cut, and was in the process of trying to even them up before she put them through the ring to begin the simple knots, when a familiar voice she had thought she would never hear again broke into her earnest activity.

"I hear you've been looking for me?"

She whirled around, a picture of swirling loveliness, as the filminess of the caftan twisted suggestively about her willowy, rounded figure and gave her the look of an exotic

149

princess performing an ancient harem dance. If the strands entwined through her fingers had only been bells the illusion would have been complete.

The insolence! In conformance with his character of the past as she knew it, here he was again, unannounced, uninvited, acting as if nothing had ever happened. Irene's anger, mixed with her almost uncontrollable, instinctive response to him, was somewhat overwhelming. She looked at him for a moment unable to speak as her senses began to comprehend fully that he was actually there.

He was dressed casually in jeans and an open-collared, Western shirt. His hair had been carelessly tousled by the wind and as always his eyes crinkled mischievously, confident that his charm would win out. He had apparently walked. Irene hadn't heard and didn't see the truck anywhere.

"You have a nerve," she finally spit out. "You broke into my home and stole my dog, and you have the nerve to show up like this!"

"I'd say we're just two up and even," he countered nonchalantly. He didn't even have the courtesy or respect to deny it. He was almost goading her!

"We have nothing to say to each other," she said quietly as she mustered herself to stay calm. "I think you had better leave."

Giving no indication that he had heard the words she had just spoken, Matt took a step toward her and with a casual motion grabbed the strands of hemp near his feet and began to straighten them. "Here, let me help you with those," he said easily as his eyes continued to examine her with warm concern.

Wordlessly Irene watched as he expertly sized the strings up and finally indicated that they were even and ready to be secured in a wrap-holding knot. "You know, Irene," he went on as if they had been companions for

150

years, "you really need to relax. Stop being so negative and believing the worst."

Unconsciously she began to wrap the strands that she held securely in her hand, sure that she was experiencing an hallucination of some kind. He wasn't there. This wasn't really happening because it simply was too preposterous.

"I want you to know," Matt continued as she ignored him, sure that he was ethereal, "that you have nothing to worry about and there is no need to pursue me, because it will accomplish nothing and, in fact, simply complicate matters. I want you to promise me that you will stop," he ended firmly and calmly. "I want you to do that. Believe me, you can trust me."

His eyes were pools of affection mirroring a care and regard that Irene had only dreamed of ever seeing. She was suddenly so confused that she was sure, more so than ever, that she was having a dream. Her yearning for him left no room for anger and her body melted as the tip of his finger softly outlined the profile of her face. She nodded in wordless assent.

As quickly as he had come he was gone. She sat stunned. It was several moments before her full equilibrium returned and she realized in fury that she had capitulated to yet another chauvinistic encounter that by its very nature was far more degrading than anything which she had endured previously.

In contempt she flung the just-begun hanger away. She was giving up too easily. There had to be something more she could do. As she headed inside with a purposeful stride she heard the zooming roar of a fast motor and saw the blur of a fast car streaking by the end of her lane, which was visible through a small clearing in the forest. There was something vaguely familiar about it, but she didn't have time to think about it now.

The telephone was ringing again, and David, who Irene had thought long lost only a few hours ago, was on the phone inviting her to a gala party he was planning for the evening before the opening of the UKC dog show.

"You'll enjoy it," Irene heard him saying in his usual exuberant way. "Plan to wear your most smashing dress, or better yet go down to the Smart Shop—you know, that exclusive shop with the resident designer, I can't think of his name, that one who hides out down here—oh, well, never mind, just choose something and charge it to me. Consider it a special gift from me. This is going to be the most elegant gathering anyone has ever seen around here. Some of the biggest dog fanciers in the country will be there."

In his usual proprietary way David was not asking, but telling her, something Irene ordinarily would not have stood for or exposed herself to on a regular basis, but she had to admit that she had encouraged him and deliberately played along, allowing him an air of confidence and delusion that was completely unfounded on reality.

As David talked on, some of their past conversations suddenly seemed to flitter through her mind and she remembered him arrogantly claiming his special influence with the district attorney's office. *I wonder,* she mused to herself, as David babbled on, not really needing any participation from her—Irene had long ago realized that David far preferred to listen to himself—*I wonder just how much influence he really does have.* It was worth a calculated risk. At this point she had nothing to lose.

CHAPTER ELEVEN

Irene still refused to believe that Matt had actually been there, that he had actually said what he had said. It was just impossible. The only proof she had was the outrageous response of her body, which had continued to tingle and reverberate for hours, and then that outlandish dream again last night, which had nevertheless left her rested, almost peaceful—a far cry from the fitful nights she had had for the past few months.

She looked out toward the ocean as she drove leisurely down the two-lane Florida State Highway 98. It was a beautiful and inspiring drive along the Gulf coast and it provided solace for her emotions after her stormy, unsatisfactory meeting with the district attorney earlier in the day. Talk about shades of chauvinism! After much beating around the bush, some of it on her part, Irene had to admit, because at the last minute she had decided that it was best not to mention David Thornton's name after all, the district attorney had had the audacity to refer her to several national animal welfare groups, indicating that dogfights were more their problem than his.

Throughout the conversation, however, Irene had sensed a certain evasiveness, and his eyes had at times seemed almost wary as she pressured him to conduct an investigation. He had been downright uncomfortable when she had inadvertently allowed Matt's name to slip. She may have imagined it, but she was sure he was more than relieved when she finally left.

Now she was on her way to meet her former husband, Jerry, in accordance with the plans she had made the day before. She had dressed carefully and was once again restored to her usual elegance. She was really glad now that this diversion had come up and she was actually looking forward to the evening, which she was sure would prove profitable to her in more ways than one.

She pulled into the drive of an elegant restaurant actually built on pilings over the water. It was completely surrounded by windows and in the twilight it was very attractive and alluring as lights danced over the water and heralded busy harbor traffic. The sumptuous atmosphere was impressive as Irene walked through the door and greeted Jerry with a smile, something which just a few short months ago would have been impossible. It was amazing, however, for all of its radiance, to realize just how impersonal that smile was.

"How nice to see you," she said graciously as Jerry made a big show of assisting with her chair. It pleased her to see that he was just a tad discomfited by her appearance and confident demeanor.

"Likewise, I'm sure," he said in overstated gallantry.

On that tone they went on with dinner almost as if they were two impersonal strangers, until Irene at last had the satisfaction of hearing him gasp when she made her counter proposal to him. Jerry quickly recovered, however, as he looked at her astutely.

"I seem to have underestimated you," he said, genuinely impressed, "but then I guess maybe I always did." He ended with a definite "older but wiser" tone.

"Perhaps," Irene said, relishing her role as the one with the upper hand, "but I'm sure we can work this out amicably."

She looked away, clearly pleased with the events of the evening as the waitress brought them dessert and demitasse. Her smugness, however, was suddenly shattered and a small gasp escaped her as Matt Davis, sophisticated and urbane, came into her focus. He was sitting across the room with an elegant, sophisticated woman of about thirty-five who even from that distance across the room exuded an air of old and comfortable wealth. Irene was sure Matt could not see her and was not aware of her presence. It was almost as if instinctive feelers had brought his vibrations to her attention.

Puzzled, Jerry looked across to her and Irene could not help but notice what a distinct difference there was in her response to the two men. If nothing else during these past few months she had, once and for all, rid herself of at least one disturbing attraction.

Her heart had begun to beat rapidly and she knew her pulse must be evident as it pounded in her throat. Slowly she commanded herself to turn away, but not before she had taken in the crisp, expensively tailored navy sport jacket and camel trousers accented with a silk navy and tan ascot. His hair was sheer, elegant perfection with the exception, as always, of that one stubborn tendril, which had become an almost certain mark of identification.

There could be no doubt. It was Matt, but never had Irene seen him so impeccably attired. He was completely immersed in his conversation as he gestured expressively over some papers he was handing to the woman. The woman, likewise, was totally enthralled with him and Irene knew she did not wish to have yet another encounter

155

with him. She was already overextended beyond endurance and she didn't need any more confusion.

Quickly she said her good-byes to Jerry and told him to contact her with the details of his offer, which she would respond to after she had had a chance to check the real-estate market in Miami. The long drive home did little to relieve her confusion and anxiety. Nothing made sense. In truth it never had, but that didn't in any way negate the fact that Rocky was missing and probably in grave danger. She continued to have the most inappropriate feelings for his kidnapper, an unscrupulous man who intended to use the dog as a pawn to gain his own ends.

There was an explanation somewhere, the most obvious one, of course, that she had simply once again fallen in love with the wrong man and she was refusing to face reality. Matt's appearance this evening was just another indication of his innate deceitfulness. It was time that she accept this once and for all.

After much soul-searching Irene decided to take David up on his offer to provide her with a new evening dress. The connotations of the offer most assuredly went very much against the grain of her independent character, but on the other hand, she was ultimately able to rationalize it as a neccessary part of her overall battle strategy.

When she arrived at the shop a few days later the proprietor greeted her effusively.

"Oh, yes, Miss Malone, we've been expecting you." There was a knowing look and meaningful emphasis in his words, which, when mingled with his foppish appearance, was decidedly annoying to Irene; but she managed to stifle her natural impulse to rebuff him and followed him to the back room of the shop.

"Now, Mr. Thornton had something like this in mind," he said grandly as he swung a sleek, elegant black confection of silk and voile out for her inspection and draped it casually over a velvet chair. He waited expectantly for her reaction.

This was too much. It was bad enough that she was letting David purchase the dress. She wasn't about to allow him to choose the style. The dress was very beautiful and would probably have suited Irene beautifully, giving her a definite, striking siren effect. It was styled with a tight-fitting bodice with a provocative and revealing strapless décolleté over a slightly flared skirt, which was covered overall with a lovely soft, sheer voile. In contrast to the silk liner, the voile was extremely demure, coming to the very base of the neckline and extending to the wrists in elegant points. It was further softened with a sprinkling of tiny hand-embroideried blossoms and fastened at the back of the neck with a tiny round silk button of the same fabric as the suggestive liner. The hemline was designed to whisper just above the calves.

Irene had to agree that the black, combined with her porcelain skin and flaming red hair, would no doubt be stunning, but it definitely did not suit her mood at the moment. She inwardly bridled at David's presumption, which he was going about in his usual arrogant and insensitive way.

"I must say," the proprietor simpered, "that Mr. Thornton certainly has excellent taste. This dress was made for you, simply made for you."

"Yes, well . . ." Irene said, not wishing to offend him, "it is beautiful and I'm sure it would be lovely on, but truthfully it is just not what I had in mind."

"Oh, well . . . certainly." The man was somewhat bewildered. "Certainly, I'm sure we have just what you may want. . . . Perhaps if you could just give me some idea . . ." He was rapidly shuffling through several racks of his exclusive dresses when suddenly a heavenly pink caught

Irene's eye. She could hear him gasp as she indicated her interest.

As with most redheads, Irene had rarely been able to indulge her fancy for pink in her wardrobe, but she knew immediately that this was a perfect coordinating shade, the exact degree of contrast that would not only be compatible with her tresses but also highly complimentary.

The disapproval of the designer was fairly evident until he somewhat peevishly held it up to her and was truly amazed by the effect. It was the kind of dress that Irene dreamed about. It suited her romantic inclinations perfectly. It was also a confection of silk and voile, but contrary to the other selection was a picture of romantic demureness obviously from another era; an era when women wore their hair up in puffy bouffants with teasing tendrils escaping, and handmade cameos were their greatest daytime jewelry delight.

It featured a high stand-up collar over soft, broad shoulders with long puffy sleeves and an overall blousiness sashed with matching material. The collar was encircled with hand-embroideried flowers as were the cuffs. The plainness of the bodice was effectively reversed with an elegant diamond pattern of matching embroidered petals. The design was intricate and must have taken hours to achieve, which was most impressive to Irene's needlework consciousness. The hemline was also descreetly calf-length. The only possible jewelry one would want to add to it would be elegant pearl earrings complemented by ultrafeminine strappy silver sandals.

It was so beautiful that Irene would have bought it in any event, but it gave her a smug sense of satisfaction to think that David was paying for it and would be most certainly disappointed when he saw it. There was no question but that this was a rather vindictive attitude; but it was one that Irene nevertheless savored for the moment

158

as she realized that this could very well be the only small sense of satisfaction that she might derive from this entire nonsensical, dangerous game she had ill-advisedly involved herself in.

As she tucked the box beneath her arm and left the store buoyantly she began once again to think about her two most recent encounters with Matt. There was something definitely disturbing about them, giving her some indefinable sense of hope—which she quickly stifled, realizing full well she was once again donning those ever-expedient rose-colored glasses simply to assuage persistent inner longings that had thus far refused to subside.

When she arrived home, however, Irene had decided that having extended herself to this extent it might be well worth her while to call one of the national animal welfare organizations, although to her understanding they had no legal jurisdiction and could do little more than what she was trying to do—with, she had to admit, very poor results. The sheriff was out of the question and she had had no encouragement from the district attorney's office. She had been afraid to tip her hand to the local humane society, sure it was impossible to know who, exactly, might be involved.

Over the weeks, in addition to everything else, David's "colorful character" friends had also regaled her with tales of what had occasionally happened to snitches, and it was obvious that such an identification could be more than a little dangerous. Ironically, though, a lot of this occurred from within their own ranks. In spite of David's insistence about the honor involved in dogfighting there was an incredible amount of petty infighting and downright distrust among the participants. Consequently, more police "busts" occurred because someone was disgruntled from within the group than for any other reason. David, however, through his menacing superiority and community prestige, seemed to have this factor completely under control in this area.

"Perhaps," Irene mused, "if I could get an investigator from the national animal welfare organization to come in, the local authorities would find me more credible." At this point she felt the authorities were treating her as just another hysterical, emotional female who was given to overreactive assumptions.

As the telephone clicked through its direct dial pattern she tried to rehearse what she was about to say. A rather impersonal voice answered and suddenly Irene was breathless and she found it exceedingly difficult to speak. Stammering, she requested someone in the investigation department and was gratified to hear a deep, warm, calm voice come through the receiver. Quickly she identified herself and tried to fill him in on the events of the past several months, describing in graphic detail David's operation and the indication that a major dogfight convention was going to take place in conjunction with the upcoming UKC dog show. The man was solicitous and exuded an air of genuine concern, but in Irene's opinion did not seem to be grasping what she was trying to convey.

"I deeply understand your concern," she heard him say in a practiced, soothing voice, "but you must understand that there is very little anyone can do in the case of a stolen animal, unless, of course, it has been tattooed and you have some definite idea of the location of the animal."

Unbelievable. It was just unbelievable. "Yes, I understand that," Irene said somewhat impatiently. "The real reason for my call, however, concerns Thornton and the big dogfight that is clearly coming down!"

"And we share your concern," the man went on smoothly, "and I can assure you that we are doing what we can. In the meantime, however, I must point out to you that these things are somewhat dangerous and shall we say

. . . at times . . . ah, delicate." He gave the last word a special emphasis, embodying it with a special innuendo before he went on. "I would, therefore, *caution* you about any further involvement. You have done the correct thing in calling us and I can assure you that we will take it from here."

It wasn't good enough. Somehow this just wasn't good enough. He was dismissing her with a practiced, gracious polish and she was receiving no satisfaction—just the usual warning to mind her own business. Impulsively Irene made one last unthinking query. "Have you ever heard of Matt Davis? Is he in any way connected with you?"

It was an outburst that she had not, in any way, planned on making. In instant chagrin she realized that her submerged, hopeful thinking was beginning to again cloud the issue.

The man paused momentarily while the long-distance line hummed emptily. Then he answered calmly and carefully, as she expected. "No . . . no, ah, there is no one . . . on our *staff* by that name." Then he spoke a little more rapidly. "As I told you, we have our way of handling these situations and I can assure you that we will do so. In the meantime I would suggest that you just relax and leave this to us. Again, I'm deeply sorry about the loss of your dog."

A second later as she hung up the phone Irene knew that she was definitely going about this in the wrong way. She would never get over Matt Davis if she insisted upon refusing to accept him for what he plainly was. The last question had been completely outrageous and she was deeply shamed over her inability to handle her emotions realistically. She sighed and once again felt deeply discouraged, but she had come this far and in spite of everyone's warnings she had no intention of quitting now.

* * *

When Irene arrived at David's estate a few nights later, Greentree was gala with festive lights and the sounds of a successful party. There was a band, dancing under the stars, and mountains of scrumptious food all elegantly served. David had gallantly sent his car for her and Irene had one decidedly supreme moment when she saw his face as he took in her appearance. She was ethereally lovely, but definitely not the striking, flashing bauble he had hoped to show off among his rich and influential friends and fellow fanciers of his beloved American pit bull terriers.

He was, as always, eloquent and gracious as he murmured over her hand and brushed her cheek in a salutary caress. "My dear, you are lovely, but I had thought perhaps the black . . ." He was so presumptuous and proprietary. It gave her real satisfaction as she answered him.

"Ah, but this is so much more the real me," she said airily. "It was lovely of you to buy it for me."

She sensed a definite touch of annoyance as David's eyes narrowed ever so slightly, but he recovered and began immediately to introduce her around.

There were at least a hundred people attending, and the glitter of jewels flashed in rainbow hues all about the room. Everyone was impeccably dressed and many seemed to be greeting and catching up with each other after a long absence. Irene easily blended in with them and to her surprise found that she was really enjoying herself, when she suddenly saw Matt and Lola enter the room.

Matt was in no way attired as Irene had last seen him. To be sure, he was in the required suit and tie, but his choice of clothing was almost dowdy in comparison to his choice of attire just a few evenings before in that restaurant in Harborville. Lola was in a flashy orchid pleated gauzy dress with a deep V-neckline that dipped to a sparkling silver belt and then dropped suggestively over her hips in a smooth line to the floor. It was garish, and Irene's original impression of a carnival Kewpie doll once again came to mind.

Seeing them together was a painful reminder of what she had forced herself to witness just a few weeks ago, and the persistent pain in her heart surfaced and gave her an immediate sense of suffocation. Feeling the need for air she quickly manueverd her way through the open French doors onto the terrace. She was immediately revived by the cool summer evening air and was once again impressed with all of the beautiful people who surrounded her.

"Do you see that elegant matron over there across the way?" David had come up behind her silently and he was now speaking with a low note of dripping sarcasm as he indicated a lovely blond woman of about thirty-five. Irene momentarily stiffened as she suddenly realized this was the woman who had been Matt's dinner partner only a few nights before.

"Yes," she said, waiting for David to go on.

"Well, she has one of the most fantastic American pit bull kennels, probably one of the best in the country aside from mine, of course," he qualified, "and she just refuses to accept the true destiny of these animals. She's a real crybaby. It's a real shame that those magnificent animals of hers have never had the chance to experience the supreme test."

It never ceased to amaze Irene when she heard David talk like this. He really was, she had come to believe, a very cynical, sick man.

"Of course, she has no idea of my true passion for these animals. She simply wouldn't understand," David went on pompously, "but it is tragic to think of such a lack of perception. But then, never mind that. I came to find you, my sweet, because I have something special for you. I had thought, of course, that you would be wearing that wonderful black creation, but nevertheless I think you will enjoy them." He had taken a small jeweler's box from his pocket and when he flipped the lid open Irene's eyes were dazzled by a lovely, expensive pair of clustered diamond earrings.

"Oh, David, I couldn't," she stammered in classic response. "The dress was one thing, but really, this is too much."

"Nonsense, my dear, nonsense, I had them made especially for you and I see no reason why you should not have the black gown also. I'll arrange to have it sent out to you tomorrow. Enjoy, my dear, enjoy." He kissed her lightly on the forehead. "I can't tell you how much I am looking forward to your supreme moment of joy when you accompany me to the regional convention, coming up, by the way, in just a few days. We planned it, you know, to coincide with this week of UKC festivities."

Yes, she knew. She just wished she knew exactly when and where, but then the latter was never known until the very last minute.

Still somewhat dumbfounded by David's extravagant gift, Irene was unable to reconfirm her previous refusal before he was suddenly whisked away by one of his guests who wished to discuss something about the UKC show with him. From the perimeter of her vision Irene saw Matt lounging in a dark corner and it was apparent that he had been watching her for some time. He must have witnessed the entire scene between her and David.

Brusquely she turned away, having no wish to have any personal encounter with him. She saw the woman David had just made reference to heading in Matt's direction. To Irene's amazement, the woman showed absolutely no recognition of him; none whatsoever. Irene turned slowly around and was openly staring as she watched the progress of the woman until she had disappeared into the crowd. After a moment Matt turned and went in the opposite direction. It was incredible.

Once again something seemed to bait Irene's imagination, leaving her confused but somewhat hopeful. Maybe, somehow, some way, all this was not what it seemed. Maybe her question the other afternoon to the animal welfare investigator had not been so preposterous. After all, hadn't he assured her . . . ?

She couldn't help a vague excitement. David had positively identified the sympathies of that woman, and Irene had positively seen her and Matt together the other evening. She was almost overcome with a great sense of joy as she realized that maybe, after all, her intuition and instinctive attraction was not . . .

But then, her ever-cautious and distrustful inner-self suddenly warned, *the woman was a breeder, nothing more, and the national animal welfare organization did not know Matt . . . On the other hand,* she reflected, again optimistic, *of course they wouldn't divulge that, not if he was in a dangerous . . .*

With that last hopeful supposition her heart suddenly plummeted again, as Irene realized just exactly how dangerous Matt's position might be. Was she, with all of her interference, unwittingly making his job more difficult? Could it really be that he was not what he seemed? Just as she was beginning to truly brighten Rocky crossed her mind and Irene was once again confused.

Surely an animal welfare group would not allow an animal to be used and abused, no matter what the ultimate gain might be—and there was no question but that Matt had Rocky, and the dog could be hurt. Irene had seen enough in the past few months to assure herself of that. You could not claim an interest in dogfighting without ultimately exposing your animal to harm. It just wasn't in the cards. Then, too, she recalled hazily, Matt had once made reference to a dog he had lost. This probably wasn't his first go-round in this arena.

No, the truth still evaded her and Irene was now honestly more confused than ever. Very probably, she finally conceded on a truly rational note, Matt was simply having an affair with that woman. He was probably a gigolo and the woman, of course, didn't wish her husband, who was probably also in attendance, to know. Dejectedly Irene realized that this rationale really did seem more realistic considering Matt's character as she knew it.

Feeling a sudden sense of tiredness she began to make her way to the ladies' powder room. To her annoyance she found herself alone with Lola when she entered. She turned quickly to excuse herself, but not before Lola beckoned her.

"Come in," Lola said. "I've been wanting to have a chat with you." This was not a Lola that Irene was familiar with, but then she had only seen her in rather extreme and abbreviated roles so she had little to compare with.

Almost as if compelled by an outer force Irene found herself turning to listen to the other woman.

"I wish you would just buzz off and leave Matt and me to do what he thinks has to be done." Lola's eyes were cold and calculating. "His involvement with that dog has never been any of your business and I for one am getting tired of your pussyfooting around in our affairs."

The intent and menace in Lola's voice were perfectly clear. As Lola dropped a small comb into her purse and closed it with a staccato click Irene realized that her rose-colored glasses had once again, most assuredly, been in action and were decidedly overworked. Lola had left her no doubt, as all of Irene's original suspicions about Matt returned and cemented themselves securely into her brain.

The rest of the evening was somewhat of a haze, but Irene managed to get through it without any further encounters. She had, in fact, even forgotten David's gift of the earrings until she returned home and discovered them in her small pearl-covered evening purse. In disgust she threw them on the dresser. She almost felt dirty as she touched them, but she knew now, more than ever, she had to continue the charade with David until she found out when and where that dogfight was taking place.

As she had known from the very beginning, she was the only one who cared, and in the final analysis, she was the only one who would ever try to do something about it. She despaired now of ever seeing Rocky again unharmed and it left a sorrow that she knew she would never lose. Irene thought bitterly of Matt Davis and knew she would never forgive him, because at last she was beginning to truly hate him.

CHAPTER TWELVE

The slow-moving mahogany paddle fan whispered above Irene as her hand moved comfortably over the frets of her small Spanish guitar and her long fingers softly strummed its gut strings. She desperately sought the comfort that this pastime usually afforded her, although it had been months since she had touched the instrument. Within moments she was painfully aware of that fact as her fingers began to smart. She settled now for just a very relaxed rhythm that had no formal structure as her thoughts ran rampant.

It was just a matter of days now, maybe only hours. She knew by David's excitement and the stepped-up activities at Greentree that the big dogfight convention was eminent, and she had reason to believe that David was waiting now for the finale of the big UKC dog show to be completed. He had entered his big Black Boy in the UKC competition and was excitedly anticipating winning a championship.

Curiously, unlike most of these dogs, which had been conditioned for the dogfight pit, Black presented no danger in the show ring arena. His training had been so finely honed that he responded to very exact stimuli and was perfectly controlled in every instance.

Logic also told Irene that the matches had to be scheduled for just after the UKC show because Black Boy was also slated to fight, and he would be in no condition for the show ring if he had recently been pitted. No matter that Black Boy would probably emerge the victor in the dogfight pit, Irene knew now that there was no way an animal could ever come out of one of those confrontations without visible injuries.

This was Thursday and the UKC show was getting underway this afternoon. Somehow she had to manuever David into divulging the time and place of the dogfight convention—that it would be late at night, she was certain, but David was so crafty that through sheer force of habit he seemed to guard this information instinctively. One of the reasons why the conventions in this area were so big—and Irene had learned that this was one of the biggest in the country—was because they were so safe.

During the past few days Irene had seen not only sleek show dogs ensconced in big vans and station wagons arriving in town, but also a number of rougher characters and their gladiator animals as well. She had seen enough big pickup trucks with gun racks to last her a lifetime, but truthfully she knew it was really difficult to discern the show-circuit fanciers from the dogfight aficionados.

These weeks with David had proven that to her. Irene was still amazed at the paradox of his existence. His kind, considerate, genteel demeanor was a well-constructed facade that camouflaged a cruel, cynical, arrogant man. Deep down inside she was truly terrified of him, but now she was anxiously waiting by the phone hoping he would call.

She had no plans to attend the dogfight. She knew she

170

wouldn't be able to handle it and there was no point if she couldn't get some help, but if she could get just a little lead time her last resort was the FBI. She was wise enough now to know that she couldn't engender very much sincere sympathy for the animals involved, but she knew there would be gambling and drugs.

In the course of her researching ways to stop the dogfight she had learned that interstate traffic was involved when the animals were carried over state lines for illicit purposes. The bottom line was that carrying the dogs over the state lines for purposes of dogfighting was against the Federal Animal Welfare Act, but that law had been little more than a farce in the hands of its enforcement agency, the USDA. Drugs and gambling would be the better bet, and she was sure the FBI would be interested.

Unless, however, she had something really concrete, Irene knew it was too dangerous, even with the help of that federal body, to tip her hand. She had no delusions about David's scope of influence. She had made a preliminary call and concealed her identity, to insure that someone would be available should she, on short notice, have a significant, worthwhile tip for them. Now she could do nothing more than wait. She was grateful that she had the solace of the guitar. Her nerves were beginning to take on the twangy characteristics of battle fatigue again.

She heard wheels coming up the drive, so she put the guitar aside and went to look out the window. A small delivery service truck from Cramdon was pulling up in front of the chalet. Irene greeted the driver at the door. He had several packages in his hands, one a large dress box with Smart Shop scrolled across the top.

"Looks like you could start your own shop," the driver joked as he handed her a clipboard with receipts to sign. "You're a pretty popular lady—only thing missing is flowers." He gave her a knowing look with a wink, and in spite of her troubled thoughts Irene returned his infectious candor with a smile.

"Thank you," she said as she awkwardly tried to manuever the packages inside. There was one large box, probably the black gown, and two smaller ones that looked as though they had come from a jeweler. "No," she said softly to herself, "not now." She had no interest in opening the packages or, for that matter, keeping them. She set them aside and went on into the kitchen, where she was just about to fix herself a glass of iced tea when her helper, Jeff, came in.

"Miss Malone, we're getting short on some of our supplies, and Mrs. Shuler forgot to pick up her Peek-a-Poo's medicine from Doc Quigley. She was about to miss her plane so I told her we would get it for her. Okay?"

"Sure, Jeff," she responded. The latter was nothing out of the ordinary. They performed such errands all of the time, but the shortage of supplies was yet another reminder of her recent preoccupation, and a little warning bell went off, reminding her to reestablish her priorities.

Within a few moments Irene was in her station wagon headed for town. She drove out of habit while her thoughts continued to buzz around. There had to be a way she could do something. She had left strict instructions with Jeff to let her know if David called. She was just pulling onto the main street when she suddenly saw a familiar truck.

As it traveled noisily down the avenue she just had time to glimpse the bulging trail tires, the flash of peroxide hair—and Rocky riding in the back, before it turned the corner and hauled out of town. She immediately shifted down and gunned her four-wheel drive as she impulsively gave rapid chase. There was no question. She had seen

Rocky and that was Matt Davis's truck. She had no intention of letting him get away.

She turned the corner and was soon on one of the narrow roads leading into the great government preserve that encompassed thousands of acres of pine forest. She could see the truck in the distance, but she was having trouble catching up. Her small engine was no match for the powerful one in the truck, but she was determined not to let it get away.

Fate was smiling on her. Her eyes filled with tears of sheer relief. Maybe, after all, she would be able to save Rocky. She drove on, concentrating solely on the truck, fearful that she might lose it as the underbrush grew thicker and small trails forked off in every direction for campers and hunters. The road was twisty and dusty. A cloud of red clay practically concealed the bigger vehicle. She quickly closed her windows and vents as the suffocating particles began to enter her car. In just that momentary diversion the other truck suddenly disappeared, having apparently turned down one of the smaller trails.

In despair she drove on as the brush grew more and more rugged. Suddenly she thought she heard something in the distance that seemed to be in the vicinity where she had last seen the other truck. Quickly she turned around and looked for a trail that would lead her to the sounds. She heard a shout and impulsively turned in its direction, but she soon found that her car could travel only a short distance on the rutted trail she had chosen.

Abandoning the vehicle, she began to make her way through the underbrush as she hysterically listened for guiding sounds, but she squelched an impulse to call out to the dog. The brambles and underbrush tore at her clothes and scratched her arms and legs, but she stumbled on, giving little regard to the pain they inflicted. She had just one driving desire—to find Rocky and get him out of there.

Suddenly she came to a round campsight clearing that was covered with long grass and had remnants of campfires in the center. The sun was a bright blaze over it and on the far side Irene saw several pit bulls straining on heavy leashes that had been staked in the ground. There were two unkempt, swarthy rednecks with them, and suddenly, instinctively, she knew that they were rolling dogs. Just as quickly she also realized that she was miles from town and in fact had no idea of her exact location. This was not a safe situation for a woman alone.

Frantically she looked around for some place to hide. Dropping to her knees, she quickly secreted herself in some thick bushes close to the clearing. She had no alternative but to wait until the men and dogs left. She steeled herself for what she was about to witness. As she settled herself, fleetingly, from the corner of her eye, she saw a flash of white lunging on a chain. In an instant she knew it was Rocky, and in her excitement she suddenly stood up, forgetting completely that she could be seen.

Just as suddenly she was jerked off balance. One of the burly rednecks had grabbed her from behind and was dragging her into the clearing. Kicking and screaming, she tried to escape his swarthy hold, which smothered her with a sweaty unwashed smell as she fought against his rough shirt. Within seconds her abductor was joined by his partner and both were leering at her with looks she had seen often during the past few weeks when David's "colorful character" friends had been rolling their dogs. Too late Irene realized that the dog was in fact not Rocky but one that just resembled him. She was disheveled and frightened. A button or two had unbuttoned from her blouse and her hair was in wild disarray.

Slowly she began backing away as the men's breathing

grew heavier in sadistic, sensuous anticipation. She realized fully what was going to happen to her if she didn't find a way to escape. The men advanced on her steadily, leering and taunting.

"Boy," one said, looking conspiratorially toward the other, "I think we oughta have a little of that. Whata you think, Floyd, don't you think we oughta have a little of that?"

They continued to advance and Irene grew more frantic, looking from side to side. She was surrounded by thick underbrush heading deep into the woods. The advancing men were blocking the clearing to the access road. There was no escape. The two of them would quickly catch her if she headed into the woods. Should she manage to get away, she could become hopelessly lost. The latter was preferable to the former so she continued to retreat.

"Yeah, she looks real sweet, Ben, ol' man," Floyd chimed in, "and she looks like she's just there for the taking."

They were so close now Irene could see the hard glitter of anticipation in their eyes as their breathing grew heavier, spacing their words. Their mouths were almost drooling. Branches pressed against her back as she felt her foot catch on something. In sheer terror she slipped and fell at their feet as their sweaty odors accompanied by low laughs filled with lust descended upon her.

Her terror was so great that she was beyond screaming or fighting. It was as though she were planted, immobile, while her eyes and senses seemed detached, watching as if the scene were in slow motion, stretching the limits of her terror far beyond the reality of the actual quick action of swarthy arms as they grabbed for her.

Slowly her reflexes began to melt, dissolving her immobility. With a final effort, utilizing all of her remaining strength, she tried to yell again. Her scream pierced the forest as she thrashed and wriggled, trying to reach the underbrush. Suddenly, just as she felt hot, foul breath on her neck and the sharp piercing pain of a branch in her back, Matt was there.

Irene saw the dark hair with the widow's peak over the dark and brooding eyes. His hair was a little disheveled by the tractor cap pushed to the back of his head. Everything grew more ominous and threatening with his appearance, yet a tiny whisper of relief also shuddered through her.

"Hey, what . . ." Matt's face registered, for just a flash of a second, alarm and concern when he saw Irene on the ground, and took in the full implications of the scene, but both emotions were immediately replaced with anger and irritation. "What in hell are you guys up to? I thought there wasn't goin' to be anyone around while we rolled these dogs. What are you doin' bringin' some chick up here?"

Stopped in midaction, the two men turned, swiveling upright from their crouch over Irene, and began to laugh a little sheepishly. "Hell, man," said Floyd as he pushed his hat back, scratched and rubbed his head, and then pulled his hat back on in an unconscious but much practiced gesture. He quickly adjusted his trousers and rubbed his belly as he leered again at Irene. "We didn't bring her up here. She was over in the bushes a-watchin' and we just figured she oughta get in on all the fun."

"Yeah, c'mon," Ben chimed in, "can't you see her there, she can't hardly wait. She wouldn'a come all the way out here unless she was a-wantin' a little fun. They's more than enough for all three of us there."

The shock of seeing Matt so suddenly, in the middle of all this, had left Irene motionless, almost in a stupor again. Now she was horrified and just plain mad—fighting mad.

"You filthy stinking swine," she spit out between gritted teeth. "You swine, how dare you . . . It's not even safe to

176

hike in the woods anymore!" She was getting herself together, punctuating her moves with words, while she pulled herself to her full height. Her nails flashed like claws as she balanced herself with a nearby tree. She tossed her hair back from her face in a wild tumble and turned to look at them, venomous and defiant. "Touch me and I'll rip your eyes out," she said through stiff lips and clenched teeth.

"Well, she is right fiesty," said Matt, seeing that the impetus of the attack was now foiled, "but man, I ain't got time to mess with no woman."

Irene's head jerked toward him, shocked, as it dawned on her that his speech pattern matched that of her attackers. He was, most assuredly, the same as the rest of them.

"I come up here to roll my dog and I ain't got all day. You wanta deal we better get with it. Besides," Matt said, looking Irene over sideways with a cynical little snarl on his face, "I got me a piece of fluff just a waitin' over there and she ain't no trouble at all."

Irene looked through the clearing to the trail. The powerful pickup truck she had been following with the oversize trail tires bulging from the sides sat there, with Lola looking away coolly, one leg propped up on the dash while she filed her nails. Rocky stood patiently and quietly in the bed of the truck.

Suddenly everything was just too much. Irene felt herself sag. Torrents of sickening pain cascaded and pulsed around her heart until she thought she would never breathe again. Truthfully, in that moment she really didn't care. She would just as soon die.

"Yeah, well . . . I guess you're right," said Floyd, his mood obviously altered. Turning from Irene, he and Ben began to walk toward the truck. "Let's get the contract done," he said, looking at Matt, "and then maybe we can all have a little party. . . . There ain't nothin' like seein'

Dutch do his stuff and then whippin' it to a woman right after . . . I reckon she can wait till we're through. . . ."

Terror returned to Irene. She had to get out of there and her car was some distance away—she wasn't sure where now. She had been in such a hurry to follow, her eyes had seen only the truck. She hadn't really noticed any of her surroundings.

Matt stood looking at Irene, shock and annoyance still evident on his face. He stepped toward her as he saw the terror overtake her again. She shrank back, horrified that he might touch her. The others were at the truck now, talking animatedly about the dogs and laughing with the woman.

"Rocky," Irene said, as tears began to trickle over her pallored face, giving it a cast of fine delicate porcelain. "You have Rocky and you're going to fight him with those swine." She broke into sobs, completely out of control. She was shaking with rage. "How could you?" she wailed. Unconsciously she had moved toward him. She raised her fists and began flailing at him. "How could you? How could you?" she sobbed, striking him over and over again on the chest.

Matt stood immobile for what seemed an eternity but was really only seconds, and then gently and firmly grabbed her arms in a deliberate motion. Irene was no match for his massive strength. She felt the hardness of his chest. Her cheeks were caressed by the tiny, dark, curling hairs escaping through the V of his rugged woodsman's shirt.

The roughness of the shirt shocked her back to reality as she pushed herself back from him, disgusted with herself. His touch should have been dirty, revolting to her, yet in the midst of all this, this horrible situation, her skin tingled. She was infuriated with herself. Slowly her eyes came up to his, masked in shame and shock. Matt was looking down on her, deeply concerned.

Hurriedly, but softly, he spoke. His hands were grasping her shoulders and gently shaking her. "Look, I know what you think and I can't help it, but you've got to get out of here." He looked back over his shoulder and saw that the men were still at the truck occupied with the dogs and Lola. His eyes, his mouth, his body, all of him seemed to caress her, to beseech her, yet he never touched her.

Irene was dazed. Everything was happening so fast—so much was wrong. Rocky was in that truck; that woman; those men; and now Matt; good, bad, she didn't know what . . .

Suddenly Matt was shaking her roughly. "Dammit," he said through gritted teeth, "did you hear me? I can keep them busy for a while, but not forever. Now get the hell out of here!" He pushed her roughly.

"Rocky," Irene cried in anguish as she caught her balance after stumbling from his push. "Rocky—I can't leave him!"

"Go!" Matt shouted in a loud whisper. "Go before they come to see what's going on. I'll take care of the dog. Trust me. I'll take care of him."

Sobbing she turned and ran. She knew she had to, but somehow, some way, she had to get Rocky before they got him to the big dogfight pit. Trust him! How could she trust Matt Davis when he was just as bad as those other terrible men?

Stumbling, Irene continued to run, unmindful of branches and mud. In the background, growing more distant, she heard whoops and shouts of encouragement. She heard dogs snarling and growling. She couldn't bear to think of what was happening, what they had done to make that gentle beast ferocious and mean; mean enough to kill

179

another dog just like him. Somehow she found her car and drove blindly until she reached the main highway again.

Once she got going, she managed to remember Mrs. Shuler's medicine for her dog and picked up the most necessary supplies, but she left the other shopping chores for later. When she finally reached home she was once again immersed in what had become an all-too-familiar numbness. She had just dropped her purse on the counter when the telephone rang.

"Irene? David here." His voice was pitched high with excitement. "My dear, I have the most fantastic news for you. You will never believe it!"

For all of her wanting to hear from David, Irene really wasn't up to it now. In fact, she didn't think she would be up to anything ever again. She was beaten and she knew it. The incident in the woods had served to shock her into understanding just how dangerous this entire travesty was.

"What are you talking about, David?" she asked dully.

"Well, it seems that friend Davis of yours *has* had your dog Rocky all along, and believe it or not, that dog came out of Carver's lines. I had no idea. . . . Seems Davis has done a hell of a job with him and a couple of our Georgia friends have talked us into tacking on a match for him."

Just when Irene was sure she had endured the ultimate in pain and despair she was piloted into yet another plane where the intensity was indescribable. She had apparently played her role with David supremely. He had no idea as to what he was doing to her as he went jovially on.

"My dear, I have a feeling that you will be proud of that animal and I want you to know that it is my intention to return him to you. I'll give Davis whatever he wants. We'll just consider it another little gift in anticipation of our future good times together."

The last had been spoken rather drolly as a familiar chill

180

racked Irene's body. She had listened silently, trying to find an appropriate response, but as always David did not miss her participation in the conversation.

"By the way," he went on, "did you receive my gift this morning?"

"Yes . . . yes, they're all here," Irene stammered, grateful that he had changed the subject. "I haven't had time to look at them yet."

"Them?" David said quizzically. "My dear, I think there should only be one, unless of course, you have other suitors as well." There was a hint of pique in his voice.

"Oh, but of course, David, it was just that several items came with it and, as I said, I haven't had time to look at them. I had to go into town for some emergency supplies we had run low on."

"Well, just checking," he said with a low, indulgent chuckle. "I can't tell you how much I am looking forward to seeing you in that gown. Well, have to go now. *Ciao.*"

The receiver clicked and the open line began to hum before Irene could respond in kind. Puzzled, she replaced the receiver and turned to examine the small packages that had accompanied the dress. They were expensively wrapped in an elegant gold paper from one of the most exclusive jewelers in town. Slowly she began to open them, wondering what they could be and who they were from.

A tasteful, small box began to emerge from one. Its contents were heavily wrapped in protective tissue. As the thin paper came away an elegant gilt head of a small owl began to emerge. It was a picture of chaste, simplistic refinement. The bottom was covered with heavy felt and it was obviously meant to be a stylish knickknack. Absently Irene set it down near the phone as she picked up the embossed card that accompanied it. She read what wide masculine pen strokes had inscribed:

* * *

181

The wisdom to discern the future belongs only to Nature and only the *innocent* shall know. Trust me. This would look wonderful on your mantel.

Matt

Irene's hands were shaking as she dropped the card and turned away. She stumbled to the couch as she tried to still her thumping heart. The other small package was clutched in her hand and she looked at it in bewilderment. Compulsively she began to unwrap it also. It was almost as if she were compelled to do so, as if someone else were doing it and she was looking on in detachment.

Within seconds her fingers felt the downy roughness of an expensive velvet jewelry box. Almost as if in a trance, she flipped it open and gasped at the sheer, classical beauty that rested there. It was a small compact brooch in the shape of a tiny miniature rosebud, which in spite of its gilt appearance looked as if it had just been freshly cut. Again she began to read the card, which was written in the same confident hand:

Wear this with the purity of intent that this metal and this blossom represents. Trust me.

Matt

The insignia indicated that it was twenty-four-karat gold, almost pure. It had just enough substance to support the shape of the bud, which seemed ready to unfurl in full bloom.

In anger, hurt, despair—everything she had felt and endured during the past weeks, Irene flung it away and collapsed into sobs. The events of the afternoon, the terrible fear of attack, further conclusive evidence of Matt's deception, David's smug insensitive, information, and now this . . . this futile reminder of what she wished might have been, washed over her. Further confused by these incomprehensible, obscure messages on the cards that accompanied the gifts, Irene could feel herself plunging into a dark pit of despondency surrounded by demons taunting her with the hopelessness of her situation. She hated Matt Davis, but more than she hated him, she loved him. These gifts and the encounter that afternoon had told her that.

In dejection she instinctively knew her own personal survival was at stake now. She would attend the dogfight and she would rescue Rocky before he got to that pit. It didn't matter what she might have to do or what might happen to her. She was going to do it. She was determined that she was going to do it. She could not survive the thought of not doing it, and when it was done she would once and for all stop loving Matt Davis. . . .

CHAPTER THIRTEEN

It was late Saturday morning and Irene was just tidying up before she left for the final hours of the UKC dog show. Jeff had agreed to stay and watch the kennel. She had managed to squeeze in only a few hours at the show thus far and she was sincerely looking forward to this time, sure that it would prove to be diversionary and restful. Rocky and Matt, of course, were not entered and it still stung to think of how Matt had taken her in.

The phone rang and as Irene reached for the receiver her hand bumped the gilt owl, which she had never bothered to move. It went rolling across the counter as she responded.

"Irene? David here. I was wondering if you were planning to come into the show today. Black Boy, you know, is going for the championship."

"Yes, as a matter of fact, I was," Irene answered tonelessly, and then rallied, remembering her continued resolve. "I'm very much looking forward to it."

"Well, you must forgive me, my dear. I had planned to call before and tell you I was sending my car around for you sooner, but I've just been frightfully bogged down with details. It's only a matter of hours now, you know, and I can hardly wait to see your reaction. Anyway, no harm done, I'm sure. The car will be there for you in about forty-five minutes. It's already on the way."

As usual, no consultation. Just sheer presumptuous arrogance. All in all David was a most degrading man. He quickly bid her farewell with his now familiar *"ciao,"* giving her no time to respond.

As she turned from the phone David's words reverberated through her brain. "Only a matter of hours, you know." No, she didn't know and she still had no idea as to where the dogfight convention was to be held. Apparently she was not going to be able to get any information that would be useful to the FBI, so she could only hope to succeed in her resolve to save Rocky. That's all she had left now.

She took a quick shower and quickly chose a tailored summer-weight linen pantsuit that still maintained its original flax hue. She added a bright kelly green silk blouse that did as much for her spirits as it did for the suit. She visibly brightened and felt much more confident. Contrasting high-heeled strappy sandals and her favorite gold stud earrings completed the outfit. Within moments she had completed her makeup and added as a final touch a gaily printed green scarf that picked up the colors of both the blouse and the suit. She used it to pull her hair back in a low chignon. She slipped a small gold ring on her well-manicured hand, replaced her watch, and situated large stylish sunglasses deftly on the top of her head so she wouldn't forget them. Giving herself a quick spray of cologne, she noted that the entire outfit was well set off by her warm sun-kissed skin.

Reaching for her purse, her fingers stumbled over the small jeweler's case that contained the brooch from Matt.

She had finally retrieved it and then thrown it casually on her dresser. Her first inclination had been to throw it away, but some inner longing that still needed to be played out willed her to keep it. Her ever-present subconscious delusions begged for a few moments to savor its beauty and what might have been, if only it had been in the first place.

Slowly, hesitantly, her hand stopped and then impulsively reached for the box and snapped it open. She gazed upon the small classical perfection of its contents. Impetuously she suddenly began to remove the pin from its satin bed and before she could change her mind quickly fastened it onto her lapel. It seemed only right that it should have its place among her memories too, a tiny symbol that would help her to remember only the best. It was beautiful on the suit and for some inexplicable reason putting it on had made her feel instantly better.

A few moments later Irene was riding in David's sleek car. As the driver pulled into the grounds of the exhibition area in Cramdon she was amazed at the number of cars there. When she went inside the entire area was a beehive of activity. There were several roped-off show rings with long rubber runners within their perimeters to indicate where the animals were to be exhibited. A large portion of the hall's space was given over to staging areas for the exhibitors. Cages, tables, chairs, and every other possible piece of canine paraphernalia were scattered over the room as owners and handlers worked feverishly to ready their entries for their next show.

The hum of blow dryers and the sounds of barking dogs were integrated with the chatter and general air of excitement that usually characterized exhibitions such as this, especially when they came down to the wire with the last championship contests. Every once in a while a general cheer would go up followed by applause as some grateful and excited participant realized the dream of a blue ribbon and trophy.

Irene finally found David's staging area, which was, in comparison to most of the others, quite pretentious. He was anxiously pacing now as he awaited the call for Black Boy's hour of triumph. The dog had already copped all of the honors in his previous classes and now he was about to go against the winner's bitch belonging to the lady who Irene now cattily and routinely thought of as Matt's rich lover.

As the call finally came for the Best of Breed competition for the American pitt bull terriers Irene suddenly caught a quick glimpse of Matt and then was stunned as she realized that he was handling the rich woman's dog. All of the winners of previous classes in this breed category were now vying for the breed championship. Slowly they circled the ring, a supreme exhibit of canine perfection, perfectly groomed and perfectly behaved.

Maybe, after all, this was why Matt had been meeting with the woman. Irene recalled now that they had been discussing some papers that might easily have had something to do with the show. But then why had the woman ignored Matt at David's party, or had Irene just imagined that? *Well, it really doesn't matter,* Irene thought to herself as her fingers absently caressed the tiny brooch.

David was standing beside Irene, a case of nerve-racking impatience. The judge suddenly made his selections in rapid succession and an oath escaped from David as Black Boy was relegated to second place. The beautiful bitch belonging to the elegant woman took first place and the championship. Matt had shown the dog magnificently and he now stood beaming and proud as the crowd applauded. As he looked across the crowd his eyes suddenly caught Irene's and she realized that he must have noticed the rosebud pin. In confusion, she wished now that she had not worn it. She fingered it unconsciously and felt such an instinctive pang of genuine regret that she was momentarily disoriented.

David's anger was more than obvious as he left Irene. He was in a fury. Irene saw him meet his handler as he came from the ring. David began to gesture wildly to the handler as the two of them continued to the staging area in deep, animated discussion. Irene saw both of them look back several times toward the offending championship bitch as the elegant woman took the dog from Matt and led her away. David seemed to give some final very explicit instructions to the handler and then left him with a resounding pat on the shoulder.

Seconds later David returned to retrieve Irene. He had recovered his usual demeanor entirely by the time he reappeared by her side. "Piece of bad luck," he muttered, "but no matter. Black will have his true moment of glory in just a few hours. If you don't mind, my dear, we will go on out to Greentree. There are just a few last-minute details yet and I'm sure you will find the prematch preparations of some interest."

David had never once considered that Irene might not wish to go to the dogfight. Incredibly, he had simply continued to assume that she was in complete accord with his rationale. Realizing that this was her last chance if she wished to end this farce, Irene took a big breath and looked around at the beautiful dogs she had just seen in the ring, and then thought once again of Rocky and his upcoming fate. She really had no choice. She couldn't live with herself if she didn't try to rescue the dog. Since Irene had pinned on the tiny rosebud brooch she had almost forgotten the role Matt was to play later in the evening, with Rocky his unwitting victim. All of it came back to her now, igniting her anger and fueling her resolve.

As they traveled smoothly in the car David patted

Irene's arm and said, "I have a surprise for you. Now that I have you alone I can tell you about what has been preoccupying me so much lately."

Irene looked at him, genuinely puzzled. She had thought at first that he was going to offer another expensive gift, but apparently not.

"In the past," David went on, "we have had to put up with the most primitive conditions for our dogfight conventions, but tonight will be different. I have just completed a wonderful underground arena tucked away in the farthermost reaches of my estate next to the government preserve. Tonight our sport will have the setting it deserves. I want you to see it before the crowd arrives."

In despair Irene realized that David had astutely waited until she was under his complete control before divulging this information. There was no way she could convey any of it, and if he had prescribed to his usual sly craftiness there would be no telephones in the arena—and the arena, she could surmise, was probably located miles from any place where one might be found.

The car seemed to drive on and on until finally it turned down a winding rutted road with the great pine forest in the background. Suddenly they stopped in what looked like an open field and then to Irene's amazement a section of the ground moved, revealing an underground roadway.

"In addition to the arena itself there is room for more than one hundred cars," David said smugly. "It will be exceedingly difficult for anyone to ever find this location," he went on, "and when we are finally ready to go public after we've had those ridiculous laws against dogfighting repealed this will be one of the finest dog pits in the world."

The car had entered the opening and Irene was immediately filled with a sense of foreboding. She was glad to see that the entry had remained open. "We still have a little duct work to complete," David said as he saw Irene looking behind, "but I'm so anxious to use the arena that we should have no problem tonight if the two entries remain open. No one, absolutely no one has any idea about this location and no one other than my people will be summoned before seven P.M., so leaving the doors open should pose no problem. Then we will make a call and everyone will come out in a caravan of cars, all of which will be safely hidden away below ground. It's ingenious, my dear, simply ingenious, and I can't tell you how proud I am that you are the first to see it." Irene could see why now, more than ever, it was so difficult to break up this activity.

As she left the car with David, she looked about with a sense of awe. They were in a great empty concrete cavern with a domed ceiling and built-in bleachers surrounding a center ring, which was the focal point. There was a vast area behind it where Irene supposed the animals would be kept as they awaited their matches. She couldn't help but compare the decided difference in atmosphere as she thought of the UKC dog show she had just left.

As David was talking, faces familiar to Irene from his compound began to come in. They began to assemble a sixteen-foot square with two-and-a-half-foot-high walls and a canvas floor. Irene shuddered involuntarily as she watched the actual dogfight pit take shape.

"Still a little shaky, are you, my dear?" asked David as he noticed Irene's reaction. "I was afraid that might still be the case, so I've arranged a little something to sort of precondition you for the big excitement tonight—somewhat of a dress rehearsal."

To Irene's horror the handlers were bringing in a pair of David's younger dogs. "Now, my dear, I don't believe I have ever explained the actual rudiments of the dogfight contest to you, so briefly the object is to test the gameness of the dogs and we determine that by how many times the

191

animal will voluntarily return to the opponent. We may not push them or goad them. It must be entirely voluntary on the animal's part. To determine that, we have what is called a 'turn,' which is anytime the dog turns his head and shoulders from his opponent. When that happens the animals are separated and they are given a twenty-second rest. As you can see," David pointed out, "they have corners just as boxers do. Then the dog that turned has twenty seconds to cross the pit and resume the attack, which is called a 'scratch.' Should the animal fail to do so, the other animal wins."

Irene was standing motionless, unable to comprehend fully what David was trying to explain.

"Very simple, as you can see, my dear, and . . . of course, as I've told you before, anyone has the right to pick up his dog and end the confrontation at any time. I thought you might enjoy just a few moments of actual combat and I must admit I rather selfishly would like to enjoy the arena for just a few moments before the crowd arrives. I've looked forward to this day for so long."

To Irene's relief, before David could gesture for the contest to begin, the handler that she had just seen at the UKC show, showing Black Boy, came hurrying in and indicated that he urgently wanted to speak with David.

"So sorry, my dear, it looks as if we are going to have to forego this little exhibition, but then, perhaps," David mused with a menacing gleam in his eyes, "we'll have an even better contest later. I'm going to leave you for just a little while, so feel free to explore until I get back."

David left hurriedly and Irene was filled with an overwhelming sense of futility. She hadn't counted on being so far out in the boondocks. From all that David had told her the dogfight matches were usually held in a barn or garage and Irene had hoped she would have a reasonable chance to grab Rocky and get him to a safe place. She was surrounded here by open fields and forest, miles and miles from other habitation. On foot she would have very little chance of success and stood a good chance of getting hurt herself as well. "Oh well, no matter," Irene sighed. She still had to try.

As she sauntered around the pit she noticed an array of pails and tubs being brought in. "What are those for?" she queried as she pointed at the large galvanized tubs. The pails were obviously for water. David had said the handlers were allowed to revive their animals, but the tubs seemed strange.

"Oh, them are for washin' the dogs," the man working there said offhandedly. "The fighters always wash each other's dogs right before the match next to the ring in front of everyone."

"They do!" said Irene in amazement. "What on earth for?"

"Oh, they's always some slick ones around who ain't above puttin' poison on their dogs' coats—kills the other fella's dog slicker than a whistle with the first good bite he gets, so they wash each other's dogs with alcohol and antiseptic and stuff."

Irene would never cease to be astounded. She simply could not understand how David could rationalize this as noble when the entire activity was laced with abuse and distrust.

She watched as mountains of food were brought in along with mammouth kegs of beer. The place was rapidly beginning to take on the trappings of any arena on game day. Before Irene knew it a general hubbub had overtaken the place and suddenly there was a great influx of people, all apparently having arrived in the caravan David had mentioned.

As they began milling around the barbecue Irene noticed that a small contingent of men had retired to the back area, where they were working with their dogs. There were lots of women and children. Many of them reminded her of folks you see in Sunday school. Their conversation, however, seemed to revolve around an element that was obviously encouraged by the anticipation of explicit violence. It was tinged with a bloodlust almost carnal in nature, fed by a hunger for unimaginable ferocity.

David was beside her again and all too soon Irene realized that her heart was about to be put to the supreme test. She anxiously watched for some sign of Matt's presence, hoping against hope that he would not, after all, be there with Rocky. To her dismay she finally saw him enter with Rocky. Lola was not far behind. Surprisingly Irene found that her reservoir of feelings and emotions seemed to have run dry. She watched calmly as Matt and Lola made their way to the back, making a mental note of their location. For some reason she had not counted on Lola being there. That meant she had to get through two obstacles instead of one. She had hoped Matt would be out front when she went to find Rocky.

Suddenly there was a general quieting as the first two contenders were manuevered into the pit. There was a general murmur of speculation throughout the crowd. Money had already begun to flash as bets were quickly made and covered. The handlers held their dogs by the scruffs of their necks as they gripped them between their legs and pointed the dogs' muzzles toward their own corners. Purposely the animals were not allowed to see each other. The dogs at this point saw only human faces and they wagged their tails in anticipation. Then those ominous words that Irene had been dreading for hours rang out.

"Gentlemen, face your dogs!"

The men whirled and turned their dogs around and the lust for attack was immediately evident.

"Release your dogs!" the referee shouted.

It became quickly apparent that the battle was to be vicious and devastating. There were none of the usual canine battle criteria—no circling or sizing up of each other, no threatening gestures or growls. Irene realized in that moment that the first confrontation way back in the beginning between Rocky and Buffy had truly been a small miracle. The attack when it came was completely mute and completely instinctive, blasphemed by the power of the dogs' jaws, which inflicted horrendous injuries. She could sense that David was becoming sensuously aroused as his hand began to creep over her in a demanding, urgent way. "My God, it's exciting," he said in a husky voice.

Irene had to admit, as she shrugged David's hands away in distaste, that these dogs were brave and tough; but that the battle was an obviously contrived travesty strictly for the pleasure of the onlookers there could be no doubt. It was evident that all of David's pompous dialogue was little more than self-serving rhetoric to support his cynical carnal needs.

As the first fight continued in mind-boggling savagery Irene instinctively knew there was nothing "natural" about this. The dogs had been conditioned, utilizing their loyal propensities, to go far beyond their natural instincts and endurance. Any natural instinctive submission or admission of defeat would end in the animal's destruction. It was an exercise in blatant depravity—there was no other suitable definition—and the dogs were the victims, betrayed because of their love and loyalty to their owners. Certainly it was a desecration of an ancient and lasting bond made between man and an animal; a direct violation of the holy stewardship man was given when it was ordained that he would have dominion over all. . . .

As Irene looked around the now smoke-filled ring, a gamut of passions both in and out of the pit was evident throughout the crowd. It saddened her to see the enthusiastic involvement of the children. While the dogs continued to battle relentlessly supporters crowded around the pit to watch intently and bet on the outcome.

Knowing she could stand no more, Irene realized the time had come to fulfill her commitment. She had sat calmly for more than twenty minutes while she suppressed an excruciating sense of nausea. She was trying to block the tragedy of the dogs in the pit from her mind as she slipped quietly from David's side. He was so engrossed with the battle that he didn't notice her leaving.

Furtively she started to make her way toward the area where she had last seen Matt and Lola. She was prepared to inquire about the restroom should anyone question her being in the area. She fully expected some sort of challenge due to the prevalent distrust among the competitors. Once again she checked out the location of the exits, which had, thank God, remained open.

She was just about to begin calling softly for Rocky when apparently the first fight ended. Almost immediately another match began. The dogs that had just battled were being brought back and Irene was truly appalled. Both were badly mauled, but one was in especially bad condition. It was the loser. As the dog began to cry out its owner went into a rage. Irene watched, horrified, as the owner cruelly dragged the dog to some unknown but, she was sure, awful fate.

Now completely frantic and sick Irene began to call Rocky in a loud whisper. Suddenly a strong hand, a familiar hand, came over her face, stifling her scream. Matt pinned the rest of her body to him. Kicking and struggling, she felt herself being dragged back into a small room filled with construction materials. A layer of straw was on the floor. She was being tied and gagged and then she heard Matt's voice admonish her urgently.

"Be quiet. Be still." It was a voice that would now, more than ever, be indelibly imprinted on her mind. Once again, as though in final insult, Irene heard those facetious words: "Trust me."

In final total despair she lay there, unable to move or scream, as she heard the fights go on—the dogs pounding on each other, flesh on flesh, magnified beyond endurance by her imagination in that dim place. She felt herself slipping into a faint, the only way left now to end the horror. As hot tears began to moisten her gag she sought awkwardly to wipe them away and momentarily sensed something strange about the small rosebud pin in her lapel. It seemed to have been damaged in the scuffle and a tiny, hair-thin wire seemed to be extruding from it.

Before she had time to consider the implication of her discovery she heard a great whirling commotion, as though some giant thing was dancing and whirling over the layer of earth that covered the dome of the arena. In sudden joyous comprehension she realized that the dogfight was being raided, as a general commotion became apparent and all hell broke loose when a police helicopter landed on the roof.

Suddenly the door to the room was flung open and Matt came barreling through it. Quickly he gathered her in his arms and loosened the binds. "I'm sorry," he said, somewhat contritely, "I tried to keep you out of this, but you just insisted." As he helped her to her feet Irene looked at him in complete bewilderment.

He turned quickly to leave. "Thanks for wearing the pin," he added, almost as an afterthought. "In the end it was what saved the day. That Thornton is really a slippery, slimy SOB." He looked at her for a second and then continued. "If you're all right I have something else that needs to be taken care of."

Irene nodded numbly, feeling as though she were nothing more than a duty-bound object of query.

"Good! Then I'll see you later, and . . . thanks again," he said as he gestured toward the brooch. There was a supreme look of satisfaction upon his face. Then he was gone.

As Irene stumbled to the door she saw the sheriff and state troopers rounding up the crowd. David was being guarded by two deputies as animals and other evidence were being confiscated. Many of the people were being spread-eagled against the wall as the deputies went over them, frisking for weapons and drugs. A pile was growing in the middle of the floor, which contained pistols, rifles, and shotguns of various sizes and calibers. The entire area reeked of marijuana as bag after bag of it was thrown along with a rainbow array of pills on a nearby table.

One older woman, well-dressed in a Dacron pantsuit, was especially indignant as she came up and shook her finger at the sheriff. "You ought to be ashamed of yourself," she said haughtily, "arresting good people like this! Why aren't you out catching the real criminals in the community." She was still blustering as she was rapidly hustled away.

In the midst of all the confusion Irene was unconsciously fingering the small damaged brooch that was still dangling from her lapel. Slowly it dawned on her, as once again her fingers touched the tiny protruding wire. She was beginning to comprehend just how important it had been.

It was hard to believe that Matt had obviously known her well enough to believe that she would wear it. Irene recalled the almost forceful inner compulsion that had compelled her to wear it. She looked at it and was saddened to see its fractured condition. As she examined it more closely she could hear a tiny, almost imperceptible hum, as it continued to home in on her location.

An inexpressible mantle of sadness settled over her as she realized how sadly mistaken she had been about Matt. Then she saw him go rapidly to Lola. They embraced in a wild hug of joy and then to Irene's ultimate surprise she saw the wealthy blond woman talking and gesturing excitedly with Matt. The woman seemed to be deeply distressed. Matt put a consoling arm around her and the three of them, Matt, Lola, and the woman, left rapidly. As they went through the door Irene saw both Matt and Lola hastily removing tiny receivers from their ears. Apparently both of them had been wired too.

Numbly Irene realized Matt had shown her no affection and little or no concern. No explanation for the roughhouse—barely an apology, really nothing. He had asked her to trust him and she had not. She remembered that last sweet, eloquent plea when he had come to her on the porch and she had chosen to ignore him. Deep within her soul she had trusted him—that's why she had worn his brooch while the diamond earrings from David were still where she had flung them three nights before. Now she had lost him irrevocably. His actions had just told her that.

In desperate need of some bit of solace she went looking for Rocky. In spite of the confusion, it took only a few moments to find him. The warmth of his square body filled her arms and his wet pink tongue caressed her face, but her heart was empty. The tears that dampened Rocky's coat were bittersweet. Although his return, unharmed, was of great comfort, Irene had a feeling of despair that she knew would never go away.

CHAPTER FOURTEEN

"Well, little lady, I guess you know you saved the day for us."

The sheriff had just stopped by to bring Irene up to date. She had been staring aimlessly at the gilt owl, which a cursory examination revealed was also an electronic bug, highly sensitive, from what the sheriff had just said.

"Being a man of the law I'm mighty sorry we had to involve you in this way," he said, pointing to the owl, "but knowing how you felt we hoped you wouldn't mind."

"But why," Irene wailed, "couldn't I have been included from the beginning?"

"None of us were, in the beginning," the sheriff said, "and then later it was just too dangerous . . ."

It had been twenty-four hours since the dogfight raid, but Irene had yet to hear from Matt. She had learned from the sheriff that Matt was, among other things, a retired, wealthy electronics executive and a voluntary special animal welfare investigator dedicated to the eradication of dogfighting. Some years back he had owned a very special American pit bull terrier that was a champion in the UKC circuit. His dog had beaten one of Thornton's dogs in the show ring. Matt had been ill and a friend had shown his animal. Shortly thereafter the dog was stolen. When they found it, it had been killed, obviously a victim of the dogfight pit. Everyone was sure Thornton was responsible. Matt had sworn himself to ending this terrible practice and this raid was just one of many he had been involved in over the past few years. Lola was from a national animal welfare organization and the wealthy blond pit bull breeder, whose name was Lydia Simpson, had been a long-time friend of Matt's.

As Irene reflected over the past few months she was beginning to doubt that she would ever hear from Matt personally. She had been a silly foolish woman, too blind to see the obvious, constantly interfering, and now she had lost him. She repeatedly wandered about the house, openly searching for memories, knowing that was all she would ever have. It no longer mattered that Matt had ultimately just been using her. His abruptness last night had made that perfectly plain. She no longer cared. She would will herself to be content with what little she had to remember. She was, by now, adept at reconstruction of her emotions.

The sheriff finished the coffee he had been sharing with her and was preparing to leave when a dark sports car zoomed up her drive. Irene gasped when she realized that the elegantly attired man who had just unfolded from it was Matt, that telltale tendril of hair still stubbornly resistant.

As the sheriff looked from Matt to Irene, he said hurriedly, "I was just leaving. Damn fine job, Davis, damn fine."

Matt smiled at him in acknowledgment, but did nothing to discourage his departure. Looking meaningfully at Irene, there was a mischievous glint in his eye as he began to address her. "Seems you have something here that belongs to me."

Irene looked at him in bewilderment and then whirled around as Rocky and Buffy burst into the room in an unholy commotion, and sudden comprehension washed over her. "Oh, surely you don't mean to start that all over again," she cried.

"Well, at least that's better than telling me the kennel is not open until ten A.M.," he said in obvious amusement.

"Oh, please, please, don't joke," Irene said, no longer able to sustain any pretense.

Suddenly Matt was across the room in two strides and he swept her into his arms. "Oh, my baby, my poor baby," he crooned. "I guess you have had more than most people could stand."

It was several seconds before Irene, in her depressed and confused state, realized what was happening.

"I love you so much. I tried so hard to keep you out of this, to protect you. I knew you would be bruised beyond emotional endurance. When I think of that slimy bastard Thornton touching you and using you for his own cynical pleasures . . ."

"But why, Matt, why?" Irene cried again. "Why couldn't you have taken me into your confidence?"

"You don't know how much I've agonized over this," he told her sincerely. "I definitely had not counted on your role in this, and then, when I couldn't seem to discourage your insistent participation, it was clear that Thornton was deliberately baiting you to satisfy his sadistic tendencies."

Irene looked at Matt genuinely puzzled.

"Oh, darling, Thornton was well aware of your feelings. He gloried in them and relished in exposing you to his unspeakable cruelties just so he could enjoy your reaction. It amused him to think that you were going to try to stop him. Had he ever thought you might actually succeed, well . . . we just couldn't take that chance. . . ."

Irene looked across the room, focusing on the wall, as she mumbled sheepishly, "Well, I guess that makes me look pretty silly, doesn't it?"

"Not at all, sweetheart, you acted like anyone who might have thought they were fighting a battle all alone, which means," he said, turning her gaze back to his own mischievous one, "Lola and I must have been doing our jobs pretty well. Although, God knows," he teased, "I did try to give you a hint or two, but clearly when you care about something you do it with such a blind devotion you are, in fact, rather refreshing."

She was slowly beginning to realize what was actually happening, and suddenly she felt as though her heart would burst as she looked at Matt's wonderful face and her eyes filled with tears.

Matt was instantly concerned. "Don't cry, baby, please don't cry. I'm sorry that I felt I had to delude you in this way, and then, when we knew you would not give up, we unforgiveably bugged you. Thornton had thrown us a real curve with that arena and we had no idea as to the possible location of the dogfight. He really kept it under wraps. I was hoping the owl would pick it up when he called you and we did get some good clues from it, but you will never know what it meant to me when you wore the rosebud. It was a calculated risk that you would wear it, but I was hoping you would pick up my vibrations. It was meant to be just a little extra insurance, but in the end it saved the day. It was a homing device as well as a bug, and the agents would never have found that dogfight pit out in that field without it. Lola and I were wired, but we could not transmit through that dome with all that earth on top. Your little pin was my own design and it worked." There was a touch of pride in his voice.

"I'm not crying, I'm not crying," Irene laughed. "I'm happy."

Slowly Matt began to caress her face softly and sweetly as his big hand twined through her hair. Then he held her at arm's length and looked at her tenderly as a chuckle escaped him. "You sure gave everyone fits," he laughed. "The sheriff, the district attorney, the FBI—they were about to have my scalp if I didn't find a way to control you, and I must say you are without a doubt the most stubborn, persistent . . . lovable . . ."—he was speaking between caresses—"vixen I've ever met."

He was slowly moving Irene toward the couch, where they had once had such a memorable few moments. "And then," he went on, wanting to clear this up once and for all, "I ended up roughhousing you. In spite of your bug the agents had one hell of a time finding that place, and to be truthful, if the doors hadn't remained open we probably never would have. When I saw you I knew the law was about to come down and I guess I just panicked. I couldn't take the chance of your trying to grab Rocky— knowing you that's what you had to be up to, and then running into the scouts and tipping everyone off before the deputies were deployed. If Thornton had gotten those exits closed we would have been in real trouble. That place would have been a fortress and they had every kind of gun imaginable in there. . . . I know I must have hurt you . . ." He sighed in mock exasperation. "I just may have to spend the rest of my life making it up to you. . . ."

Too late Irene realized that this must be yet another incredible dream. In her agony she had finally flipped out completely—but the great warm canine tongue that was suddenly rudely interfering, and the perpetual wriggling bodies of her two impertinent dogs, assured her that this was really happening.

"Speaking of Rocky . . ." Matt said speculatively.

An involuntary gasp escaped Irene before she could squelch it. It had in truth become almost a reflex action, as her pathos and concern for the animal over all of these past tumultuous weeks continued to take its toll.

"Relax," Matt said laughing. "I have no intention of ever taking Rocky from you. He's had a pretty rough time of it already. We rescued him from another dogfight raid last winter. His owner was trying to sell him. That's how he got those botched ears and that tail—oh, yes, that tail," he said in exasperation. "You know, when you came on the scene I wasn't ready to clue in the sheriff yet. Too many times the local police are involved in the dogfights, especially when something is as big as this operation was, so when I saw things weren't going well with the sheriff I just happened to have those United Kennel Club catalogs with me. I had honestly forgotten about that tail standard—it really is in the fine print you, know. Then later I realized that if I could make my peace with you, working with Rocky here at the kennel could provide a good cover *and,* more importantly, by that time I think I was already falling in love with you and I was manuevering subconsciously to spend as much time with you as I could. I guess," he sighed, "it was fairly obvious that Lola wasn't too happy with me . . . but then I was also beginning to realize as you became involved with Thornton that you might be in *real* danger, and I felt responsible for your safety." He paused with a grimace as his long fingers began to again twine through her long hair. "Later when you discovered Rocky was disqualified because of his docked tail you caught me completely by surprise. I was so angry and frustrated with myself for forgetting such an obvious thing—I don't know what came over me. I knew I was going to lose you and I just had to touch you one last time. . . ."

Irene was listening to him patiently, trying desperately to get all of this straight in her mind.

"Of course, you know by now that Lola was working with me. She may have gotten a little proprietary, but she is a good animal welfare agent and plays her role well. . . ."

With a pang Irene remembered the night at the motel. Reading her thoughts, Matt lifted her chin and looked into her eyes. "And for what it's worth I wasn't staying with her in the motel. Didn't you hear my car roar away that night?"

Irene's eyes widened in embarrassed surprise.

"Oh, yes, my honey, I've known every move you've made. I really was worried that you were going to get hurt. That's why I came to see you that day on the porch. In a way it was a foolish thing to do, but I was almost half crazy with worry over you. You are so stubborn! I wanted to tell you I loved you that day. You looked so lovely and exotic. I knew deep in your heart you loved me too and it grieved me knowing how much I was making you hate me. I had no alternative when I took Rocky. I needed him as my cover. To make this bust we had to infiltrate the actual fight. There was no other way to get in. If they didn't know you personally you had to prove yourself by participating. Thornton was one of the biggest organizers and one of the worst. He is a powerful, sadistic man and it was important to nail someone of his caliber. He knew something was up but he felt secure with his arena and he didn't suspect that you could actually harm him. I think he was blinded by your innocence and his lust for you. I surmised that he had terrible plans for you and then I discovered evidence that you probably would not have been his first victim. After I learned that I decided to send you the bugs, not only to help with the raid, but to protect you as well."

He turned to her earnestly as he held her firmly by the shoulders and willed her eyes to meet his again. "I want you to know that Rocky was never, ever abused in any way. We did nothing more than hint at the inbred potential that these dogs already have. I sincerely did nothing to encourage it. The other contenders were well aware of Rocky's lack of conditioning and just agreed to that match out of sheer greed. Rocky was too young in the first place. I want you to know that never would I have allowed Rocky into that pit. I would have forfeited if the raid hadn't come down."

Finally, as the whole scenario was beginning to sink in, Irene could feel just a touch of anger beginning to revive. "But you left me last night! You showed no concern, no consideration, and now here you are just the same as before—on bended knee with a smile on your face, unannounced, uninvited, acting as though nothing serious has taken place. You really are too much!"

"Well, I suppose," Matt said in a husky, calculated voice, "you could always have me thrown into jail."

Once again he had managed to turn the tables on her and Irene looked at him in genuine puzzlement.

"Bugging your house and person was more than just a little illegal, you know, and I suppose if I don't shape up I could have that hanging over my head for the rest of my life too."

"Too." The word had a glorious sound to it. In spite of her resentment Irene found herself laughing in abandon as Matt joined her and pulled her to him in a long soulful kiss that had its origins in eternity.

"I am sorry," he said after a few moments, "deeply sorry. You should never have been left like that, but Thornton had Lydia's dog—you know, the lady who owned the champion bitch. We just managed to rescue her dog before Thornton's handler turned that monster of a dog, Black, on her. It was like living my own nightmare all over again. I just had to save that dog and I knew you would understand. . . ."

Irene did, indeed, understand. In that moment she loved him more than even she would have thought possible and she berated herself silently for all of her petty, resentful thoughts.

Then Matt laughed as he pulled her close and kissed her tenderly. He gently nibbled her ear and nuzzled her smooth shining hair while his tongue began to track the edges of her ear. "I'll never forget that night when we almost made love. I wanted you so much and I thought I had lost you for sure," he whispered. "You'll never know how often I've dreamed of that night."

At the word dreams, Irene felt herself beginning to blush, but she continued to look at him intently. As if on cue he pulled her to him and began to gently massage her neck and shoulders in a repeat of that earlier ill-fated scene.

Then a flash of genuine anger clouded his face as he gently held her an arm's length away. "Then after all I'd done to protect you, when I found those creeps about to attack you in the woods . . ." He sighed. "I'll never know how I kept from blowing the whole operation right then and there. You can truly thank Lola for diverting their attention, but I'll spend the rest of my life making sure you are never in danger like that again.

"And now, Miss Malone," he said, suddenly taking on an authoritative, serious demeanor, "what would you think, since you obviously love chalets so much, of spending your honeymoon in an authentic original in the Swiss Alps?"

Irene blinked at him, sure again that she must be dreaming. Before she could answer Matt went on to further enlighten her. "My full name, by the way, is Matthew

Davis Evans. We shortened it up so Thornton wouldn't readily recognize me. Although it has been more than five years since I lost my dog, Rex, I have a distinct feeling now that Thornton remembered and was playing games with me too. . . . But in any event, I just thought you ought to know that your full name would be Mrs. Matthew Davis Evans." He looked at her, waiting expectantly for her reaction, and was amused by her momentary bewilderment.

Irene turned to look at the sleek car in the drive and realized it *was* the one that had passed her at the motel that evening and the same one that had spirited him away on that hazy incredible afternoon not so long ago. When the sheriff had told her Matt was a wealthy electronics magnate it had barely penetrated her mind. Now she realized from what he had just said that Matt was the owner of the huge conglomerate Evans Electronics. He could probably buy and sell her little operation a thousand times. Before she realized it she heard herself stammering irrationally, "But my kennel . . . my business . . ."

"Your kennel, your business, of course I wouldn't dream of taking that from you." Matt laughed, obviously delighted with her confusion, as she tried desperately to comprehend. "We're going to be very happy here—that is, if you want me," he said softly, "but I thought we could both use a little rest and relaxation and the Alps are beautiful this time of the year . . ."

Irene was completely beyond words as she fell into his arms and nodded joyously. "There are still more David Thorntons out there conducting dogfights every weekend all over the country," Matt said on a serious note again. "Although not much more than a fine will probably be given to Thornton, he at least knows he no longer has carte blanche to act any way he wishes. I'm afraid we still have a long way to go as far as the courts are concerned in these cases, but since you seem to be so persistently inclined to interfere," he said impishly, "the kennel will make a fantastic front while we continue our battle against this activity. We can begin," he ended meaningfully, "by donating those diamond earrings to the humane society."

Irene realized in genuine amazement that Matt had indeed witnessed her scene with David on the terrace and was jealous, but his voice was also filled with an emotional huskiness and a comforting possessivness that she realized was what she had been missing all this time—someone who cared, someone who truly cared about her as a person in every way, someone who cared enough to cherish her.

When they turned at last into a long-awaited fulfilling embrace Matt suddenly swooped her into his arms and looked toward the bedroom, with the wide bed and the beautiful forest glen behind it, evident through the high chalet windows. Irene was still in her rumpled kennel clothes from doing her morning chores. Realizing how very much she loved him and wanted him, she also wanted this to be a very special moment. Matt's lips began a fiery trail down her neck and he began to nuzzle the loosely closed buttons on her blouse, seeking the softness of her breast. Irene moaned and then gasped as she breathlessly whispered, "Matt, honey, please, I want you so much, I want to be with you forever, but I also want to be beautiful for you. . . . Give me just a moment to bathe and change. I've been in the kennel all morning."

"Honey, you are beautiful all of the time and I need you now. I've waited so long." Gently he dropped with her to the bed and his fingers began to remove her blouse leisurely as his lips lightly caressed her eyes and then buried themselves in the great tumble of her hair. "Seems to me, as I remember, one of the most exciting things I've ever seen was you in that wet T-shirt trying to cover yourself

211

with that towel. God, how I wanted you then! You were an absolute tease."

"Tease," Irene cried, as suddenly the comedy of that situation became apparent to her, "I was just trying to look decent in front of you!" she laughed.

"Oh, you looked decent all right, decent enough to eat!" He joined her in laughter as they began to lovingly tussle on the bed.

"Well, just you never mind, Matt Davis," she said in mock consternation, "I'm going to love you like you've never been loved before, but I'm going to be clean when I do it!" With that she gave him a playful shove and went bounding out of his arms toward the hot tub. Quickly she dropped her clothes and turned to stare at him, fiery and defiant, as the steaming water began to gush into the tub. In sensuous bump and grind tradition she grabbed a towel and came toward him as he watched her in startled, mesmerized fascination.

"All right," he said, drawing out the syllables, "let's take a bath!"

Within seconds they were in each other's arms as Matt's clothes rapidly joined hers in a pile on the floor. As his strong hands traveled over her slim supple body he once again swung her in the air as they both settled into the tub with the swirling, steaming water surrounding their embracing bodies. Slowly their hands began to explore every titillating possibility as their touches fired the intensity of long, deep kisses. Gasping for just a moment, Irene turned from him and began to languidly pin up her long tresses, leaving teasing strands to frame her gamine face. Her eyes were impish as she watched him take in the undulating movements of her breasts. He moistened his lips and looked at her in absolute wonder as teasingly she reached for the perfumed soap and slowly began to create a great mound of foamy aromatic lather. Suggestively she reached for him as her long tapered fingers began to slowly massage the lather into his hard, lean body. Her eyes never left his as she felt his nipples harden beneath her magic fingers. Their lips touched tenderly and then dissolved into a hard, urgent demand. Matt's strong arms went around her as he reached for another bar of soap. Their tongues parried in carnal delight as slowly he began to lather her entire body. He pulled her into his lap as his hands slowly encircled her navel and moved over her thighs and whispered lightly through them, leaving Irene gasping in delight.

"Oh, more, Matt, more," she sighed, as his hands continued their magic. Instinctively, as she lay back in absolute heaven, her soapy fingers reached for him and felt the delight of his urgent strength, growing ever stronger, wanting her. Matt's lips continued to trail over her, seeking out her breasts, and he pulled her to him urgently while his fingers continued their flickering delight until he brought her to a gasping release. Slowly they came together in a teasing oneness. Irene felt his strength pulsating within her, urging her on to further ecstasy. Then suddenly in one great final motion Matt pulled her to him and swept her into his arms as he carried her from the tub. Setting her down gently, he wrapped her in a bath sheet, which Irene quickly released and flicked over him lightly. Then with a gasp of desire Matt pulled her once again to his throbbing manhood as they fell onto the bed and became one in an unending, soaring crescendo.

As his lips caressed her body and settled on the sweetness of her breasts he moaned, "I love you, Irene, I love you." And Irene knew at last that this was no dream, as she whispered over and over again her love for him, too.

CHAPTER FIFTEEN

At the last moment, Irene wondered if she was doing the right thing. She glanced around the bedroom, which was strewn with clothes and luggage, while she sat completing the last-minute touches to her appearance before leaving for the church.

"What's the matter, honey? Having some second thoughts?" Matt had come to the door and he spoke to her reflection with an impish grin on his face.

Irene, momentarily flustered, willed her eyes to meet his in the mirror. She swallowed and with all of her remaining courage she attempted to answer him candidly. "To be perfectly honest, in a way I am," she said, as a shaft of pain shot through her in unison with his instant loss of humor. He looked at her questioningly. "Oh, to be sure," she went on rapidly, "there is no question about my love for you, or yours for me, but then . . ."

"But then what?" he said with just a touch of annoyance as he stepped into the room and turned her face to meet his gaze squarely.

She looked at him, deeply sorry for the confusion she

215

was suddenly feeling. She could feel the beginning hint of tears as her eyes grew shiny and reflected the hurt in his. "It's just," she said, willing herself to continue, "that, well . . . I know I shouldn't bring this up today, but I loved Jerry, my first husband, too . . ." She wrung her hands nervously. "I never thought anything could go wrong. I guess I took my matrimonial vows with him almost absently, and suddenly as I'm sitting here getting dressed I realized just how fragile those vows really are and . . . I'm scared."

"Oh, honey," he said, as his humor returned with a chuckle and he dropped to one knee and met her gaze levelly, "you're just having a little stage fright. I love you and you love me. We understand each other and communicate perfectly with each other. No two people could be more right for each other."

Their eyes met in an eternal communion and Irene felt an easing of her tensions as the majority of her fears dissolved.

She reached for small pearl earrings, and the diamond on her left hand sparkled and reminded her of just how much satisfaction it had given her when Matt had ceremoniously slipped it on her third finger just a few weeks before. His eyes traveled with hers to the ring. "Putting that ring on your finger was one of the most joyful experiences of my life," he said, as he brought her hand to his lips and continued to search her eyes.

Irene was surprised at just how much it had meant to her. She had thought she was not a person who had to have valuable tokens so long as the thought was there, but somehow the size and sparkle of that diamond did much to reassure her symbolically of his lasting affection.

But now her hands were shaking and she couldn't seem to still them as Matt continued to watch her. She picked up the tiny rosebud brooch, restored once again to its original beauty, and thought of how she had worn it that day of the raid in an almost unconscious communion with him, not knowing that the intensity of their true feelings was a guiding beacon for both of them. Never had Irene felt this way about anyone or been so happy as she had been in these past few weeks, but an old echo seemed to be intent upon persistently encouraging this nagging paranoia.

"Baby, this is our day to be happy," Matt said, giving her a gentle shake. "We've planned everything just the way we wanted it. Now, I know by old traditions I shouldn't be in here right now," he continued as all of his perennial impishness returned, "but I'm telling you now to hurry up, hustle your bustle, and put a smile on your face or I'm not going to give you a chance to wear that beautiful dress down the aisle of that church. I'm going to put that bed over there to use," he said with a lascivious grin as he gestured toward it, "and you could remain a fallen woman forever!"

Unable to resist his ever-ready teasing and humor Irene burst into laughter, shattering the promise of depressing tears as they turned into drops of happiness. She stood up slowly and slipped her feet into beautiful linen pumps and surveyed the dress she had chosen so carefully for this day as she met his flashing eyes.

It was not in any way like the one she had worn in her first wedding. To please Jerry, she had been very chic and modern that day, but secretly she had always been disappointed at the lack of nostalgia, as they were married by a judge in a posh country club setting. Today was going to be different. Matt had wanted her to have her heart's desire in everything and they were having a small wedding in an old-fashioned church in the middle of Cramdon.

"Here, let me take a look," he said. His words were still tinged with humor as his hands reached out to turn her gently about. "Now that I'm here maybe I can help with a zipper or something." He winked as he gave her a playful pat on the bottom and then kissed her sweetly and gently.

She was a picture of nostalgia, but nevertheless completely in stride with current styles. Her dress was a natural-colored lace and linen design that featured a small, close-fitting lace bolero jacket with long narrow sleeves, and a plain, calf-length linen camisole with spaghetti straps and a slim dirndl skirt of matching lace over it. The hemline, with a ten-inch border of scalloped lace, whispered beautifully around her sheer hose.

In complete awe, Matt stepped back and noted with approval that her hair was swept up in calculated casualness, allowing just a wisp or two to escape. He watched as she pinned a small matching pillbox hat into place and looked around for her flowers. Seeing them, she seized them and took one last backward glance in the mirror. She was pleased with what she saw.

Then, taking a deep breath, she stepped into his arms and feigned adjusting his boutonniere as she looked into his admiring eyes. He opened the door and they went out of the chalet together. As Matt opened the door of the sleek black car he paused and turned to her once again. "I love you, Irene," he said, "and I always will. Nothing can change that."

The look in his eyes told her she was definitely doing the right thing. Together they went to the beautiful old church. When a few moments later they repeated the words love, honor, and cherish, Irene knew at last that her dream had come true and it would last forever.

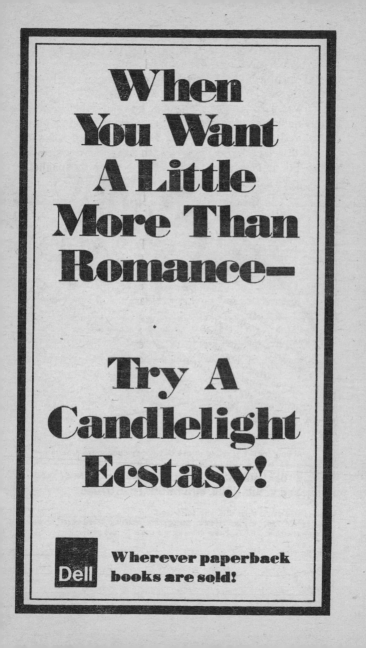

VOLUME I
IN THE EPIC
NEW SERIES

*The Morland
Dynasty*

The Founding

by Cynthia Harrod-Eagles

THE FOUNDING, a panoramic saga rich with passion and excitement, launches Dell's most ambitious series to date—THE MORLAND DYNASTY.

From the Wars of the Roses and Tudor England to World War II, THE MORLAND DYNASTY traces the lives, loves and fortunes of a great English family.

A DELL BOOK $3.50   #12677-0

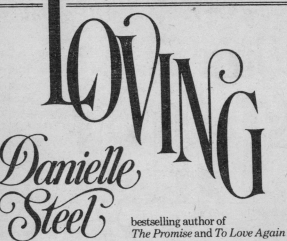